Mystical Science

By Harlowe Frost

Printed in the United States of America: First Printing, 2023.

ISBN: 978-1-959981-20-6 (eBook)
ISBN: 978-1-959981-19-0 (paperback)

http://www.hannahwillow217.com

Copy/Line Editor: Angela Grimes
Editor: Weslee Imrisek
Formatting: Huckleberry Rahr
Cover Art: Getcovers.com

Coastal Wolves:

1: Pacific Pack

2: Wolf Magic

3: Campus Prowl

4: Loan Wolf

5: Pack Triage

6: Mystical Science

7: Lupine Investigation

Novella

8: Honey Moon

Dedication:

This book centers around two scientists. One of my editors has a science background, which I leaned on heavily. I am incredibly lucky in everyone who's agreed to help me on my journey, from my alpha readers, editors, to my ARC team!

As always, this book wouldn't be what it is without the blood, sweat, and tears (most of the tears are mine) of Weslee Imrisek and Angela Grimes. They turn all my writing from chicken scratches to gold. They know how much I love and appreciate them.
And then there are the readers. Without you, I wouldn't have the inspiration to keep spending hours dropping words to digital paper. You warm my heart by reading my stories.

Thank you!

Chapter 1 - But You Can't Stay Here
Mazzy

Mazzy sat at her desk, looking over her notes. She'd been studying the increased healing properties of werewolves. "Is there a way to utilize their altered genetics to aid in healing non-werewolves without turning them?" she mumbled to herself.

After a few moments, she took a deep breath, realizing she'd slowed down her breathing as she'd focused more on her work than anything else around her. Her sigh echoed through the lab.

This part of the compound, a small subsection of Sunrise Pharmaceutical Research and Development, worked mostly off the books. They generically did 'research', but their division never produced tangible results, at least nothing the company could take to their stockholders. Since Sunrise Pharmaceutical was owned by the pack—her pack—she wasn't worried about the stockholders, even if the majority were normal humans who knew nothing of werewolves.

Her table was covered in books, notebooks, and a tablet. She also kept notes on a computer. She cross-referenced records with historical references to werewolf healing. From what she found, hundreds of years ago, werewolves healed only slightly faster than humans did. It was only in the last two and a half centuries that the healing abilities of werewolves had improved.

She looked at a second book. About a hundred and fifty years ago, a group of humans had discovered the wolves and started to hunt them. The number of packs diminished by almost half. Suddenly, it was like the wolf spirits that inhabited the werewolves began to figure out how to heal faster to survive—a sort of evolution.

As always, Mazzy was lost in the world of wolves long gone who had learned to adapt to save the species.

The lab door opened with a click. The sound jerked her from her work. "This better be important," she snarled.

"Do you know what time it is?" She turned to see Miguel standing there, a look of exasperation on his face. It was a look she was used to from her alpha.

She checked her watch. "Nine-eighteen."

He dropped into a chair near the door and pushed off the floor, rolling over to her. "Mazzy, our job goes from nine in the morning until five at night, five days a week. We fought the board hard for reasonable hours. You staying here, night after night, to all hours, defeats all our hard work. Go home."

"Is that an order?"

"No, you know it isn't. Here, we're colleagues. I know I'm your alpha, but that's never played a part here." His voice sounded strained.

She slumped. *That wasn't fair of me.* "Sorry, boss. You're right." She pushed back from the table. "I just get lost in the work. It fascinates me."

"I get that, I really do, but what's the rush? You're studying things from years ago ... our ancient history."

"I know, but some of it may help us understand how things affect us today." His brow rose as he gave her a look, the same skeptical look she got every time she got sucked in by her pet project. She relented. "There isn't any rush, I just ..." She sighed. She didn't have an answer. "Fine, I'll pack up and head home. I'll continue tomorrow morning."

"Afternoon."

"What?"

"You work late every day. Come in late. You've put in plenty of hours. Take the morning off."

She narrowed her eyes.

"I'll play the alpha card if I have to."

She sneered as she started closing everything down—the computer, tablet, and lights—and put the books away. "Sometimes I really don't like you, you know that, right?"

He smiled wide. "Nah, you love me. Should we have lunch together tomorrow before you come in? I'll take you out for Thai."

Rubbing her eyes, she shook her head, laughing at how excited he sounded. "Fine, lunch. Text me the address."

Mazzy got the last of her project secured before following Miguel out. He gave her a hug, holding her tight before they each went to their separate cars. He had his wife at home, and she had ... well, she had a home, a cat, and dinner to make.

I have the mysteries of the past. What more do I need?

Chapter 2 - Sit a Spell
Caroline

Finals were finally graded and recorded. Caroline had a month to pretend she wasn't a professor, didn't spend her days working with teenagers, and to not think about spending half her evenings grading papers. She loved her job, but she also loved time off to relax.

She headed over to the coven's headquarters. Now that school was out, she wanted to spend some time on magic. The historical Victorian house centered Caroline. She loved having a place all the witches could call their own. The coven had bought the house from the family of a deceased former member. Her husband had been the werewolf alpha, and they'd lived here, since witches weren't allowed to live in pack house. They were even discouraged from entering if at all possible. Whatever its history, Caroline loved the house and its location.

The main floor had a great room with a living room, a dining room, and kitchen. Down a hall was a master bedroom with ensuite. The second floor had three bedrooms and the laundry. Two were assigned; one to a now former student of Caroline's—Katt, a freshman from Colorado. Now that she finished her finals, Caroline hoped for more lessons *from* Katt on the Power of Seven, an antiquated magic system. Katt came to Santa Cruz knowing little about covens but a lot about different magic systems. The young woman could do magic Caroline had only heard of but never seen in practice.

But the basement, that was the best floor of the house. The former owner had created a kitchen for brewing spells. It wasn't a skill all witches had, but Caroline was an expert. It came close to chemistry, not her best science, but as a general rule, she knew science.

She headed down the stairs and consulted her notes. She had a cup of poisoned sweet tea. One of the local werewolves had been targeted by black witches, who had poisoned her stock of homemade sweet tea at her office. The concoction didn't seem to affect the wolves, but it caused deadly heart attacks in witches and humans.

Caroline wanted to combine what she knew about chemistry with magic to find a counter spell. Because her specialty was biology, she'd had to try a few times to get everything correct.

This was her third attempt. If this didn't work, she'd call in Katt and see if the Power of Seven could solve the problem.

She selected her ingredients and got down to business.

Lost in the magic and science, the hours melted away. Ingredients had to mix and cook. She stirred constantly, observing as the colors changed. When the opaque liquid turned clear, she turned off the Bunsen burner to let it cool.

She reviewed the spell, practicing the lines a few times quietly to herself to make sure she knew the exact wording.

Caroline took a deep breath, then let it out slowly. Standing over the clear liquid, cool to the touch, she recited the words. *"A binding of strength. Black to break. Heart to heal and soul to mend. Curse to end."* She chanted the words thrice.

A blast of magic left her and she slumped, then stumbled to the couch. She wouldn't have to wait long to determine if it worked, but she did have to mark time for her energy to return before she did any more magic.

Footsteps above let her know someone else was around. A knock on the door preceded the door opening. "Hello?"

"Yeah, I'm down here. Cinthia, is that you?"

"Caroline? It's me. I was checking on the house. Anything interesting down there?"

Caroline let her head fall back on the couch to watch as the coven leader made her way down the steps. "I mixed a new brew to counter the concoction the black witches are using to cause heart attacks in people. I was going to test it once I figured out where all my energy went."

Cinthia chuckled. "Have you eaten anything today? You seem to like magicking without sustenance."

Caroline grunted. "During the school year, I'm on a strict schedule. School just ended, and my schedule is still wonky. I'm sure I ate something before coming over."

"I'm not." Cinthia turned on the stairs. "I'll be back with a sandwich, and then we'll test out your mixture."

After a few minutes, Cinthia returned with a couple of ham and cheese sandwiches and mugs of tea.

After they ate, they took a tablespoon of the sweet tea. Caroline ran the tests necessary to ensure the concoction was still active. Once confirmed, she added her potion. She held her breath as she imagined the fight between the two spells.

And in this corner, black magic, fighting for chaos and death.

And in this corner, white magic, pure and good, trying to clean up the mess of the evil.

She bit back a giggle. Cinthia raised an eyebrow at her as she took a sample for testing.

"Fuck!" The black magic sludge was still present.

Cinthia sighed. "It didn't work?"

"I need to talk to Katt. The next step is the Power of Seven."

Chapter 3 - As Long As You Know Who's Boss
Mazzy

Dennis, the menace of apartment twenty-seven C, knocked a book from Mazzy's pile next to her bed. She'd decided five would be the maximum for that pile. The rest stayed on her bookshelf.

Her eyes shifted towards the edge of her bed, but she couldn't see the book—not without sitting up. "You have twenty minutes until breakfast. I know I'm usually up by now with a cup of coffee. Don't worry, you won't starve. Even if I'm in bed, you'll get your food."

With a haughty look on his face, her orange roommate tried to perch on the stack of remaining books.

Mazzy rolled over and sighed. *So much for sleeping in.*

The cat landed on her shoulder, paws hitting her like mini ramrods. Dennis stomped his way down her body and then back up.

Get a cat, they said. They're sweet companions. My ass.

"Mroww!"

"All right, you pain in the ass! I'm getting up!" She tossed her blanket off, dislodging the eleven-pound monster, and trudged to the bathroom. "Just because you woke me up, doesn't mean you'll be fed any earlier than your normal scheduled breakfast," she snarled.

He followed her into the bathroom, winding his way through her legs, demanding pets. "Give me five minutes, you demanding beast!" She bent and scratched him behind his ears, giving him a long stroke down his back. He arched up, purring loudly in appreciation.

Once she'd finished in the bathroom, she changed from pajamas to jeans and a purple, long-sleeved T-shirt with a black cat holding a mug of coffee in one paw and a knife in the other. Along the bottom it said: *Some Mornings it's Hard to Decide.*

As she slipped on her socks, the cat's auto-feeder activated, and Dennis darted from her room. *Finally, a few moments of peace and quiet.*

Mazzy headed to her living room, carrying the book that Dennis had knocked off the pile. A mystery. Her pack kept suggesting she read books with werewolves, witches, and vampires ... or other paranormal creatures. The inaccuracies about werewolves annoyed her. Anything with witches made her skin crawl. It wasn't that she despised witches, she just would rather avoid them. And the rest? They weren't real. She'd rather lose herself in a story that, although fake, was still grounded in reality.

At eleven, her phone vibrated. She had to dig it out from under Dennis, who'd curled up on her lap. A snarl vibrated up low from the cat's belly, letting her know exactly what he thought of her invasion of his territory. A text with a time and address. Lunch with Miguel.

Mazzy loved her pack, and Miguel was a fantastic alpha. She wondered if he'd bring Alice, his wife. Since it was a work day, and she worked at Sunrise Pharmaceuticals as well—but on the human side—Mazzy doubted it.

The hidden werewolf division only housed her, Miguel, Thomas, Kaitlyn, and Gus. The challenge to hide five werewolves and the LRD—Lupine Research and Development—from close inspection was a quarterly battle. When the company was created, LRD was a small department created to house research for a team of up to seven people. They tried to keep the team small because it was easier to fall under the radar with fewer people.

She had just enough time to get to Saim Star. She should've guessed Miguel would pick his favorite spot for Thai food despite its distance from work. When had practicality ever been his top priority?

The host led her to a table. To her pleasure, all her workmates were there. Happiness bubbling within her, she sat at the empty seat between Alice and Gus. She narrowed her eyes. "Shouldn't you all be at work?"

Gus laughed. "What, you think you're the only one who gets some time off and a free meal?"

Mazzy rolled her eyes. "I just wanted to get back to my research."

"Of course you did. I'm just waiting for you to set up the lab and do some massive experiments. You're doing all the historical research ... are you trying to take over my job?" Gus shook his head, amusement bubbling from him.

A shiver ran down her back. "Gods no!" Everyone at the table laughed. "You and Thomas can continue doing all the reading.

Kaitlyn and I will run the lab. But have you read any of these books? It's fascinating."

He shook his head. "You can dazzle me with what you've found ... at work. For now, figure out what you want to eat!"

"If you can tamp down Mazzy's excitement on whatever her current project, I'll ..." Kaitlyn's voice trailed off.

Thomas snorted. "You'll what?"

"I don't even know. I can't imagine Mazzy being distracted from work. It's not even a thing." Her face scrunched up in confusion.

The waitress came over, and they ordered. If the woman was shocked at the amount of food, she didn't show it.

Miguel leaned back. "Kaitlyn, plans for this weekend?"

"I'm heading into the mountains to go skiing. We only have a couple weeks until Christmas, which means the hills are about to get crowded."

Thomas tilted his head. "Want a partner? That sounds fun."

"Sure." Kaitlyn raised her Thai iced coffee in a salute, then took a sip.

Alice knocked her shoulder into Mazzy. "Are we on schedule to go to the soup kitchen or to tutor students studying for their finals this weekend?"

Mazzy smiled at her alpha. It was amazing to her to find a pack that understood her so well. "This weekend, tutoring. Next weekend, the soup kitchen."

Gus narrowed his eyes at her. "Do you ever socialize? Date? I know I've asked this before, but you should think about adding people outside the pack to your calendar."

The food came before she needed to answer him. *Why do they always push me? I am happy with my life. I have an excellent pack, a fulfilling job, an obnoxious cat, and volunteer work. Why do they all want me to do more?*

Chapter 4 - Queen of Spades
Caroline

It was Wednesday and Caroline didn't have to get to bed early for classes. It was only a week since classes ended and she wasn't yet in the groove of winter break. That didn't mean her friends and coven weren't working to get her into vacation mode. Cinthia would be around to pick her up any minute.

The kitchen sink was piled with both last night's dinner mess and this morning's cereal bowl and coffee mug. *Meh! I'll clean it up later. Who's here to complain? The joys of living alone.*

She patted her pockets to make sure she had her phone, then grabbed her purse. The keys hung from the side pocket. Once outside, she locked the door, skipped down the stairs, and headed to the sidewalk to wait for her coven leader.

Within moments, the old Volkswagen bug pulled up to the curb. Caroline slipped in and buckled up. "I can't believe this car still functions. The magic is strong with you."

"Magic and a great mechanic."

Caroline smiled at Cinthia. The older woman still dressed as if she wished the sixties never ended. Long flowing skirts, a peasant blouse, a few necklaces, dangling earrings, and a scarf wrapped around her waist with dangling beads.

Cinthia pulled away from the curb and a few turns later merged with traffic on a main street. Caroline leaned back. "Where are we headed? You wouldn't tell me before."

"A coffee shop."

"Really? At this hour?"

"Calm down. Cafés serve other things besides coffee. You can get a nice tea and maybe a muffin." Cinthia smiled, her eyes on the road, not Caroline.

"Okay, that's fine, but why are we going to ... does this place have a name?"

"It does. It's called the Zesty Bean. It's the coffee house near the pack house."

Caroline rested her head back. "Are we meeting Tamsin or any of her wolves?" Caroline liked the alpha of the local werewolf pack. They worked together at the University of California - Santa Cruz, UCSC. Caroline was a professor of biology and Tamsin taught in the English department. Though there wasn't much overlap, they'd found reason to socialize while working in the same institution.

"Yes, we're meeting Katt and Jett. Now that they aren't your students, I thought we could all sit and talk. And maybe something more."

The 'more' intrigued Caroline. Although the two weren't her students at the moment, they could end up in one of her classes again.

Cinthia parked, and they got out. Katt and Jett had arrived before them. They sat at a table with mugs and pastries. When they got to the front of the line, Caroline ordered a mug of mint tea and a slice of carrot cake. She took her order to the table and sat. Jett smiled at her warily.

Katt sipped her drink as Caroline took a bite of her dessert. "Did Cinthia tell you what this was about?"

Before Caroline could answer, Cinthia sat with her own tea and a muffin. "I did not. Now, Jett, did you bring cards? You aren't going to cheat, are you? Can you smell when we have a good or bad hand?"

"Hand?" Caroline gazed around the table, excitement building. "What are we playing?"

Jett finally smiled a wide, real smile. "Spades. Since Katt is sitting next to me, you'll be her partner. Do you know the rules?"

On the one hand, I could lie, and see how far it gets me. On the other, werewolves can smell lies, right? That's a thing. What to do, what to do.

A smile stretched across her face. "I'm familiar with how the game goes."

Jett narrowed her eyes. "Oh, you're one of those. I see, I see." She shuffled the cards.

Caroline shifted to look at Katt. "I was hoping tomorrow or Friday we could have a lesson on the Power of Seven."

Her eyes widened. "Break just started and you want a lesson already?"

The cards landed on the table, one by one.

"I've tried mixing my spell to counter the black magic concoction three times, and it's failed every time. I think I need to do something with the Power of Seven. I'd like to work with you. I know you've taught me a lot—"

"More than anyone else. You're a fast learner and more interested than anyone besides Cinthia." Katt cut her eyes to their leader, who just smiled.

They all gathered their cards.

Cinthia sighed as she started to arrange what she held. Caroline gazed at her own cards, trying to decide how many of the thirteen tricks she could take. The game was a combination of strong cards and finesse, and she knew she was skilled at both parts.

"I can take three tricks." She put her hand down, wanting to watch everyone's faces. *Can I pick up on any tells?* "So, will you be willing to assist me, say tomorrow?"

To Caroline's left Cinthia narrowed her eyes at Jett, her partner. Together they'd need to take the total number of tricks they bid. "I can take two."

Katt closed her hand and put the cards down. "Sure, let's say after breakfast? Maybe nine? And I can take five." *My three, her five. Eight. We're in for a big pull. I hope she knows what she's doing. Yikes!*

Jett watched everyone as they bid. "Huh, three to me." She tilted her head to the side and smiled. "That's interesting. Well, I guess three it is, then."

Caroline wondered who at the table didn't know how to bid. She worried it was her partner.

As a smile spread on Jett's face, Katt grumbled, "At least I know I can help you with the magic, if not this silly game!"

Chapter 5 - Decision Made, Can't Be Undone
Tamsin

Tamsin sat on the side of her bed and watched Paige prance around in nothing but her skimpy undies. She gathered clothes for the day, but until she got dressed, the other woman's beauty and grace were worth a moment of appreciation.

"Stop gawking at me, or I'll come over there, and then we'll be late."

Tamsin leaned back on her elbows and chuckled. "Nothing can happen until we get there, so, technically I can't be late. I say you glide that sexy body of yours over here and let me have a taste ... or three."

Paige casts a glance at her over her shoulder. "You already had a nibble this morning. We need to get out to the kitchen where the others are waiting."

"Hmm." Tamsin made a questioning sound. "But what if I want more? You're a submissive wolf and my mate. Isn't your position to make me happy?"

She guffawed as she sashayed over, straddling Tamsin's lap. "My job," she leaned down for a kiss, "is to make the pack a saner place." She wrapped her arms around Tamsin, pressing her chest in tight. With a wink, she rested her forehead against Tamsin's. "I'm not your personal happy-maker."

Tamsin ran her hands down the silky, smooth skin of Paige's back. "Are you sure?"

The other woman trembled and then sighed. "I'm sure." She leaned in for one more searing kiss. "Now, love, I must put on clothes and go get some coffee. You have a job to do, and making Mildred and Tory wait isn't very nice."

With a gusty sigh, Tamsin fell back on the bed, letting Paige go. Paige giggled as she got up and headed to the closet. When she emerged, she wore jeans and a fitted black T-shirt with the words: *Be Kind!* on it in rainbow letters.

Getting up, they made their way to the kitchen. They found a group sitting around the table which was stacked with plates of bacon, eggs, toast, and sliced fruit. They each selected a mug and filled it with coffee before joining their packmates.

Tory, petite and energetic, smiled wide. Her dyed blue hair practically glowed. "It's about time. I worried you'd fallen asleep."

Georgette, on her other side, snorted. "I doubt sleep is what they were doing."

Tory rolled her eyes. "I know, I just prefer to think of Mom and Mom sleeping, and not doing other things. Don't ruin my innocence."

With a mock-shocked look, Georgette let her jaw hang open for a moment. "Please tell me you and Mildred do more in bed than just sleep. You're a nurse, you know about the other things you can do, right?"

Everyone laughed. Maria, across from Georgette, shook her head. "This from you. The woman who refuses to date. Do *you* know there's other things that can be done in a bed?"

Maria and Georgette had been razzing each other for as long as Tamsin could remember. Both were about seven years older than her; she'd idolized them when she was a kid. Though not actual sisters, they acted enough like siblings that it was hard to remember most days they had different parents. The fact that Maria's parents pretty much raised Georgette didn't help.

"Just because I don't feel the need to run out and find a mate doesn't mean I'm ignorant."

Tory raised her hands. "Enough. Stop. All of you need to stop right now. Gah!" Mildred had her hand over her mouth. She looked close to exploding with laughter. "Tamsin, is this happening today?"

Tamsin leaned back and considered Mildred. "Are you sure you want to do this?"

"I am. I've been training every morning for a few weeks. I've asked a lot of questions of Tory. I know what I'm asking for. I think I know what I'm getting myself into. And," she looked at Tory, and her face softened, "I really want this."

"Then yes, I'm ready. I'll take her into the backyard with Maria and Georgette, and then I'll bite her."

Tory half-rose from her chair. "What about me?"

"No."

"What? But I'm a nurse. Yes, me."

"Trust me, Tor. You care too much. It's hard to see someone you care about get hurt. Once I'm done, Georgette will come back in and collect you. But for the initial bite, it would be too hard for you to watch."

The smaller woman shut her eyes, and Tamsin could see her fighting back words. Neck straining with her frustration, Tory nodded in acceptance. Tamsin was her alpha, and it was always hard for the young woman to go against the alpha. Tamsin hated using that fact, but this was important.

She looked over at Mildred's plate. "Eat up. Your body will need to do a lot of healing today. That takes energy, and energy means food. I know you've been told your appetite will increase. It's time to start eating more. Here and now."

"Okay. Thanks for the reminder." Her hands shook as she lifted her fork and continued to slowly eat her food. She suddenly chuckled. "I hope I don't ruin my bikini body."

Everyone laughed at her joke to help her relax. Her nervousness was obvious.

Once breakfast was finished, Tamsin took the selected few out to the backyard. Maria and Georgette stayed with Mildred, going over the procedure with her one last time while Tamsin shifted.

Tamsin's change to wolf hurt. The shift was swift, but the process of bones shrinking, hair receding, and body morphing, wasn't pleasant. Once she'd put on fur and paws, she shook, stretched, and walked a lap around the backyard, moving all her muscles.

It was mid-December, and the scents were changing. She took a moment to take them in, enjoying her enhanced senses. She couldn't imagine what it was like to be human and nose blind.

After the weeks of morning training, Mildred was acclimated to wolves. Tamsin noticed a small smile on the woman's face when she saw Tamsin as a red wolf.

"Okay, lie down on the ground and expect pain." With a wry grin, Georgette sat down beside Mildred, who chuckled. Georgette asked, "Do you want to hold one or both of our hands?"

"No. Well, maybe. Yeah. I just feel really exposed wearing only a bikini. Is that weird?"

Maria sat on her other side, and they each took one of her hands. It had the extra bonus of exposing her flanks ... sides, and hopefully preventing her from punching Tamsin.

"The outfit is to make Tamsin's job easier. It's also because anything you wear would need to be thrown out." Maria gave Mildred a small smile.

Mildred stiffened, then nodded. "Right, the blood. I guess I should've thought about that." She squeezed her eyes shut. "Okay, um, can we just get—"

Tamsin attacked. She bit down on Mildred's side, making sure her saliva mixed with the other woman's blood.

Mildred gave a small squawk of fear but then whimpered instead of screamed. It hurt, but it was pain she wanted and was ready for. They'd prepared her well.

Knowing that doing this twice would be awful, Tamsin moved to her thigh, gave a quick chomp, then backed away.

Maria had some bandages. They wouldn't be needed for long, if everything went to plan, but it was a psychological thing.

Tamsin slipped over to her clothes. There was a bucket of water for her to rinse her mouth off first. Then, she let her humanity back out. Once she had skin instead of fur, she slipped on her jeans and shirt and rejoined the others.

Georgette had gone into the house to collect Tory while Tamsin changed. When Tamsin walked over, Tory smiled up at her. "She's healing. It worked."

"Perfect. I'm glad. Mildred, you don't have to join the pack, you can decide after the next full moon in January. But until then, welcome to the pack."

She winced as she sat. "Thanks. I do plan on joining, I think. Right now, I'm just focusing on breathing, though it *is* getting easier. My head is spinning."

"Talk to Paige and Cyrus. Then Connie. They're the most recent recruits. They'll be able to help you the most."

While the three of them continued to focus on Mildred's healing in the backyard, Tamsin headed into the house. She found Jett and Katt in the living room, along with Paige and Georgette.

Paige gazed up with concern in her eyes. "How is she?"

Relief and joy flooded in from the wolves in the backyard. "Healing. She'll be fine."

Paige slumped. "Good. I'm so glad. I'm going to make sure her transition is so much better than mine."

Paige had been attacked by the former alpha's best friend, an insane wolf who thought changing a journalist would somehow protect the pack. He'd stalked Paige and nearly killed her one night. She'd awoken in an unfamiliar room. The next thing she knew, the world of fantasy creatures was real, and she was smack dab in the middle of crazy town.

It wasn't until Tamsin returned to Santa Cruz because of the death of her aunt that Paige had been brought to the pack house and met the rest of the pack.

Georgette snorted. "Not a high bar."

Paige shrugged, shaking her head. "Fair, but you know what I mean."

Tamsin sat next to her mate. "Anyway, I wanted to talk to you all about the black witch problem we're having and the poisoned sweet tea."

Katt leaned forward, elbows on her knees. "Oh?"

"Yeah. There's a research facility out in Colorado."

Paige perked up. "Oh! You told me about them when we talked about the mate connection. They do research on anything and everything werewolf."

"Exactly. I want to email them and tell them what's going on. We have so much information at this point. Maybe get some of the concoction to them for study."

Jett scoffed. "You want to mail them poison? Like, through the U.S. mail?"

"No, I was thinking of driving it out there. It's only a couple days to get there. And it's winter break. I think my job can spare me."

Georgette tensed. "Your job can, but can the pack? Tamsin, you just returned to us. Please tell me you aren't going to leave."

Tamsin massaged her temples. "If not me, then who?"

Chapter 6 - Help to Some, Help to All ...
Maybe
Mazzy

Dennis head-butted Mazzy on her ear. She snarled at him. He purred back at her. *Do regular people without orange beasts get to sleep in? Is that a thing?* With a sigh, she gave up on pretending to sleep.

She flipped back her covers and trudged to the bathroom. After a quick shower, she prepared oatmeal and coffee.

Dennis sat, staring at her. She narrowed her eyes at the cat. "Your food will come when it comes. Same time every day. Stop trying to control me with your cat brain! It won't work."

As always, she assumed her arguments fell on deaf ears. He just yawned. Leaning over, she scratched her companion before she headed into the living room to curl up on her favorite spot on the end of the couch. Dennis followed, perched on the top of the couch, and purred louder to remind her he was there. "You won't starve, drama king, it's only a couple of minutes."

Why do I try to reason with him? It's not like he understands me. Hell, I'm talking to a freaking cat! I must be mad.

Dennis swatted her to get attention.

"Already, you spoiled beast." She reached up and gave him some love while she checked her phone for any updates.

A few minutes later, the feeder made the sound he wanted, and he ran.

"I knew you were only after one thing," she grumbled. "Using me, that's what you're doing."

Once Mazzy finished her food and coffee, she returned the dishes to the kitchen, washed them, and put them away. Then she wiped down the counters and did a general clean up. She gazed at her tidy space and sighed contentedly. *The joys of living alone.*

She patted her pockets for her phone, grabbed her purse with her keys, and then locked up on her way to meet Alice.

The two were heading to a local tutoring center near three campuses. After navigating her neighborhood, Alice turned into traffic. "Do you know if all three schools are still in session?"

"I think one had finals last week, but at least one has finals this week. We should have a few students who need our help."

Alice smiled. "Your help. You know science and math. At this point, very few need help with English. Their papers were probably due last week."

"You can help them with Spanish."

"True. Miguel keeps pushing our house to be bilingual. If and when we have kids, he wants them to know both languages fluently." A glow came to Alice every time she spoke of her husband.

"And what do you want?"

She checked her mirrors, and she merged right. "The same. Knowing Spanish is becoming more and more important in this country. I think if our kids are fluent in both, a whole slew of career opportunities will open up for them."

"True. But if they're scientifically-minded and stay in our pack, there's a good chance they'll work at the lab with us, no?"

Alice's face scrunched up. "Maybe. I don't want to make any assumptions for my kids. There are other packs, and even the option of not being affiliated with a pack. There's a whole wide world out there. No reason to assume any kid will stay homebound and packbound."

The car went silent for a bit while they both contemplated Alice's words. Then Alice continued. "Look at you. You're originally from out East. You relocated here."

"Well, yeah. That's because of the lab and the research done here. There's nothing like it. The Colorado lab is infamous amongst all the packs. I knew as soon as I heard about it I had to relocate and work here." A warmth blossomed in Mazzy at the memory of being accepted by Miguel and his pack.

"Well, we were glad when you showed up on our doorstep. Kaitlyn is an amazing scientist, but that lab needed two. I mean, if we had a third it would be even better."

"Another chemist?"

"Naw, physicist or biologist. Something different to broaden what we can do. You and Kaitlyn are enough for chemistry. If we threw in a third there would be World War Werewolf. The two of you already have big enough opinions. But a new variety of scientist would be lovely."

They pulled into a parking lot. Although half the spots were covered with snow, there were plenty available.

Inside, the room was set up for the tutors to have one area and the students to sit in another. Mazzy and Alice walked over to one of three long tables along one wall for the tutors. Perpendicular to these were smaller areas where students worked. Mazzy put up a sign that read: 'STEM.' She figured she could manage just about any of the basics. Anything else, as long as the student had good notes, she could probably muddle through with them to figure it out.

The first student, a young man in a state school sweatshirt and in desperate need of a shower, had a physics question. They worked together for half an hour determining how to figure out which formulae to use and how to pull information from application problems. He then took his work to a separate table. He promised—or perhaps it was threatened?— to return.

After he left, a young woman in a green and red sweater with a Christmas tree on it sat down across from Mazzy. Her brown hair was pulled back in a braid, and she wore a headband with antlers. One sniff and her hackles went up. The earthy, herbal stench told her all she needed to know. A witch. Though Mazzy knew her to be a witch, witches had no known method to identify werewolves. Mazzy cut her eyes to Alice who smirked and shook her head. Mazzy's distaste for witches was well known in the pack.

"We're here to help everyone, not only some." The alpha's voice was so soft, Mazzy knew the student wouldn't hear.

Mazzy spoke a bit louder. "I'm pretty sure it's time for my break."

"We just got here," Alice replied with some authority.

The girl's eyes got wider as Mazzy spoke with Alice. The girl said, "If you can't help me, I guess I can Google my question. Do you not know chemistry?"

The accusation hurt, but the student had given her an out. "Google, perfect!" Mazzy agreed.

"Or ... maybe I could return after your break. I'm just having trouble with Googling a solution as well. It's this organic chemistry assignment. I lost a few points, but I'm not sure why. The professor's explanation didn't make sense."

Mazzy scrunched up her face. Chemistry was her specialty. She majored in it and then went on to get a master's degree. She loved organic chemistry. Gritting her teeth, she took a breath and smiled at the girl. *Be pleasant, Mazzy, show Alice how nice you can be.* "Please, sit. I'm sure we can figure this out." Kill them with kindness, right?

As she perused the sheet, everything looked correct. The witch's work looked good. She got to where the professor had marked points off, and Mazzy knew exactly what had happened. She rubbed her temples.

"Look, right here. You reversed your symbols. I'm guessing it isn't about your understanding, it's more to do with writing and working too fast."

The witch's eyes widened. "Oh, my gods! Why didn't I notice that before? Why didn't my professor? It's such a small mistake, a typo really."

"I don't know, for either of you. My guess is, a stack of papers to grade and not a lot of time to grade them. Now, if you don't mind ..." She waved her hand towards the student tables.

"Oh! Of course." The student blushed before heading back to her seat.

As soon as she was seated, Mazzy let out a long breath.

Alice shook her head, her own math student heading back to her table after being helped in calculus. "Did that hurt you?"

"What?" Mazzy rolled her eyes.

"Helping that student?"

"Maybe, a little."

"You do know the war between witches and wolves is over, has been for years. In most areas there's peace, they get along. Some have even mated."

Mazzy dropped her jaw in mock shock. "Gods above, say it isn't so!"

Chapter 7 - Power of Seven
Caroline

Today's game of cards had Caroline rolling. As good as Katt was as magic, her skill set didn't transfer over to cards.

Katt sneered at the cards on the table. "You ate me out!"

Jett bit down hard on her lower lip, squeaking, despite her valiant attempt to hold back her laughter.

Cinthia reached over and touched Katt's arm, her face tight. Caroline recognized the look as the coven leader held back a laugh. "Dear, the saying is: 'You ate the queen.'"

Katt's wide eyes met the coven leader's as she blushed. "Gods, I'm never going to learn this silly card game. Can we go back to Spades? Hearts is just weird."

A snort escaped Jett. "No, you're doing great. Really. Amazingly great. This is maybe my favorite thing, like, ever."

One of Katt's eyebrows rose. "Favorite? I thought that *other* thing was your favorite thing." Despite Caroline not thinking it was possible, Katt's face turned a brighter red.

Caroline threw her head back and howled with laughter. "You two were not this fun in class. I like this side of you, both of you."

Jett gathered the cards to shuffle, smiling.

A knock came to the door. Cinthia rose and glided over to the entryway. "Tamsin, Paige! We didn't expect to see you today." She looked over her shoulder at Jett. "Did we know they were coming over?"

Jett shook her head. "I didn't know."

Cinthia faced the alpha and her mate, stepped back, and swept her arm in welcome. "Enter in peace."

"Thank you, Cinthia. I enter in peace and hope for nothing but tranquility for you and yours." Tamsin bowed her head and then entered.

Behind her, Paige bowed her head as well. "Thank you, Cinthia. I enter in peace as well. I wish you peace and tranquility."

Cinthia moved to the open-concept kitchen area and started the kettle. "Tea, coffee, something stronger?"

Paige sat at the kitchen island. "It's three in the afternoon on a Monday. Something harder?"

Caroline moved to sit next to her. "It's winter break. What do days or time even mean?"

She winked. "True. I'll have coffee."

Tamsin sat in the dining room. "I'll have coffee, too."

Katt sighed. "I'd prefer tea, if it isn't too much."

"Not at all." Cinthia set up a platter with a selection of tea and then placed it on the table beside Tamsin. "Jett?"

"Coffee, please. And thank you."

As Cinthia continued to gather beverage items, Tamsin got up and sauntered in to help. "Do you have cheese, crackers, or other small finger foods?" She poked around in the cupboards.

"Of course, dear. You know your way around the kitchen."

The two moved around the kitchen like dancers on a stage. Caroline loved to see them work together. Tamsin's aunt and uncle used to own the house, and she wondered how often Tamsin and Cinthia cooked a meal with each other. They made it look seamless.

A few minutes later, everyone was sitting around the dining room table, drinks and food at hand.

Tamsin leaned back. "I was wondering if you had any update on the *concoction*. Any overall thoughts."

No, damn it! Am I able to get this done? I hope I'm up to the challenge.

Cinthia nodded as if she'd guessed the other woman's reason for visiting. "We've been working on an antidote, but so far it hasn't worked. Caroline, do you want to add anything?"

After a moment to clear her mind of her negative thoughts, Caroline put on her teacher's face. "Sure. I figure the concoction the black witches are using involves magic. That's why it can't be replicated. So, I've been trying to determine a spell as well as use chemistry to counter whatever they did."

Paige's eyes almost glowed with interest. "Has anything worked?"

"Not yet." Caroline slumped, scrunching her nose in frustration. "The magic takes a lot out of me. Despite my wants, I can't test things more than two or three times a week. After my third fail with traditional spells, I asked Katt for help with the Power of Seven. She's been training me. Her instinctive understanding is brilliant."

Katt scoffed. "I wish I had the rest of my books. I should've gone home to visit my parents during this break, but with everything going on, I haven't arranged it yet."

Both Cinthia and Tamsin gazed at her with an identical 'leader look' that meant they were trying to figure out how to solve a problem.

Tamsin shook her head sharply. "Do you think this Power of Seven will work?"

Katt sighed. "It isn't the end all be all of magic, but there are nuances that could wiggle in to break up the black magic where traditional methods are failing."

"Good, good. That's all we can hope for. There's a research center with a lot of antique historical records. I've contacted them. I haven't heard back, but I'm hoping they can help as well. But, until then, please continue doing what you've been doing. I know I don't have any right to tell you what to do, but if you can figure this out ... please." She sipped her drink.

"Of course!" Katt nodded. "It's one of the reasons I'm still here."

Caroline felt pride in her former student and now mentor. "Katt and I have plans to continue until we figure this out ... *if* we can figure it out." *We better be able to figure this out. The black witches will come after our coven, and I don't want to know I could've stopped the loss of more life and failed.*

Chapter 8 - Not All Research is Theoretical
Mazzy

A collection of notebooks lay open on the table in front of Mazzy. Some were hers and some were historical records from the archives.

If our healing evolved in a time of need, could our evolution include a means to heal others? There has to be a way! None of her research pointed to a way to use werewolf healing for others. Her lack of progress wouldn't stop her digging. She punched the desk in frustration.

From across the room, Kaitlyn sighed. "Please, don't destroy our equipment. What did that poor desk ever do to you? Just take a break."

Standing, she paced the large, state-of-the-art-lab Miguel built for her and Kaitlyn. She rolled her head, trying to think of something new. *I have to get out of my head.*

She got to her desk, a dark walnut work surface in the back corner she rarely used. With a sigh, she turned on the computer. The pack had a robust email and messenger communication system. Mazzy rarely checked either. She forced herself to check her email about once a week, just in case there was something important ... there was *never* anything important.

The few times there were, Miguel or Alice knew to text her.

Once the beast of a machine was booted up, she navigated to her inbox and saw there were massive numbers of emails. With a sigh, she methodically went through each sender, deleting the junk mail, and scanning the notes from the pack. After an hour, she discovered a message from Tamsin Hath, alpha of the Pacific Pack from Santa Cruz. Mazzy froze.

Oh, shit! That came on Saturday. Okay, it's Tuesday. Only three days, not that bad.

She leaned forward and opened the email.

Dear Members of the Colorado Research Center –

My name is Tamsin Hath. I am the leader of the Pacific Pack. I was hoping for your assistance with a situation we are facing in Santa Cruz, though I fear it could eventually spread beyond my territory.

At some point this last summer, a group of black witches came to town. We're not sure of their exact time of arrival, but we do know that they aren't limiting their attacks to either spiders or wolves. They've created a concoction that mimics heart attacks in their victims. The number of deaths has mounted to the extent that even regular humans are beginning to ask questions.

We have a sample of the concoction and are currently working with the local coven to find a counter spell, but we're hoping for help from you and the expertise all of you represent.

Thank you for your time,

Tamsin Hath

Mazzy read the message again. *Why am I in charge of the outreach email?! It won't get emails, they said. Well, what's this?* Hands shaking, she picked up her phone and called Miguel. "We need to hold a meeting."

The pack gathered in a conference room around a large, oval, redwood-stained oak table. Mazzy stared at her Sunrise Pharmaceutical Research and Development colleagues and nodded. "Okay, everyone. There's an issue in Santa Cruz. I received an email from the alpha of the Pacific Pack; you each have a copy of what she sent. I'll give you a minute to read it over."

Once done, she stood. She had too much energy to stay still. "What they're facing may align with my current research. They need an antidote for this concoction, and if we can find a way to utilize werewolf healing, that could make all the difference."

Gus shook his head. "Do we know that this concoction doesn't affect wolves? You're making a pretty big assumption."

"I agree that some of your research seems to align with this," Kaitlyn said. "You've been studying healing, and I believe you have some books on magic in there as well. But you shouldn't fixate on just that."

Mazzy flopped back down in her seat. "No, nothing I have right now focuses on witches. Not yet. I'll start adding that in. Gus, Thomas?"

Thomas held a blank face as he said, "On it."

Alice laughed. "You and your discrimination against witches. You're going to have to get over that, you know."

Not anytime soon. "No, but I'll have to include them into my research."

Thomas turned to Gus. "Okay, so we'll have to start studying black witches and their history."

Miguel clapped. "Sounds like we have a plan. Thomas and Gus, books. Kaitlyn and Mazzy, chemistry. Alice is over with the humans, and I'm here to be pretty."

Gus threw a ball of wadded paper at him. "You need to work on that 'being pretty' thing, if that's your role, boss!"

Miguel waggled his brows. "Mazzy, email Tamsin back. Ask her for details about what they've already done. It says they have some of the concoction. We need that. Some of her wolves will need to visit. Extend an invitation."

She tilted her head. "You're the alpha around here; shouldn't you send the email?"

"Nah. You got the email, you should reply. And yes, that means you'll be checking email every day until those pack wolves arrive."

She narrowed her eyes. "Why are you punishing me, boss?"

"Because you refuse to come to my Christmas celebration every year, and I'm guessing this year won't be any different."

She gaped at him as the others laughed.

Chapter 9 - A Trip to Plan
Tamsin

We welcome you and/or a small group from your pack to join us in Colorado to further discuss your situation and study the concoction. Our pack is at your disposal, as is our research facility.

Mazzy Sinclair

Sitting at the dining room table, Tamsin closed her phone. She searched the faces of the members of her pack. *Gods above, when did it get to be so big?*

Dinner was one of the few times everyone gathered together, and this was a rare meal when both Connie and Tory were off from work on a non-full moon night. As a pack, they took up the entire dining room and a few people even had to eat in the kitchen.

She leaned back and tapped her knife on her glass. All the separate conversations around her quieted. "I've heard back from the Colorado research center. They're interested in helping us. They need some of the concoction to really dig in and study it."

Georgette snorted. "Are you going to mail the poison through standard mail or certified?"

Maria knocked into her shoulder. "You know you have to declare liquids, especially poison. Make sure you don't tell Bexlee; she'd need to take you in personally."

Bexlee laughed. "Should I start the paperwork now or wait?"

Tamsin sighed. "Okay, okay, enough already. We've been invited to send a small group out there. The question is, who?"

Talking erupted from everyone. Several people had ideas and theories as to who should go and who should stay.

Finally, Tamsin whistled to get everyone's attention. "What I meant to say was, who will be traveling with me?"

Georgette snarled. "Really, Tam? We finally get you back and you're ready to leave already?"

Tamsin held up her hand in a stop sign, but Georgette wasn't done. She could feel Georgette's ire as her friend's dominance and frustration flowed through their connection.

"No, I'm not kidding." She pushed her chair back, face hard. "I know you think we'll be fine with you half a country away, but things are crazy here. Black witches, death, new pack members." Georgette's hands waved as she spoke. Next to her Maria nodded, agreeing with her. "You are our alpha. You need to stay. I'm sorry, no, you can't go. Choose others. I'd go, but I'd be useless there. Bexlee would be good, but she probably can't take time off from work."

With a sigh, Tamsin rubbed her eyes. "Anyone else have an opinion?"

Jett raised her hand.

"You don't have to do that here. We aren't in class; just speak up." Tamsin tried to bite back any exasperation.

"Both Katt and I are off school until the start of January. And Katt knows the magical side of things."

Tory leaned back. "That's true. But I know the medical side, as does Mildred."

Their newest wolf nodded, though she looked a bit overwhelmed in the full group.

Paige snorted. "Mildred was just bitten a couple of days ago. She shouldn't leave the area until after her first full moon. I know that isn't for a few weeks and everyone *should* be back by then, but we're talking Colorado in winter, they could get snowed in. I may be from California, but I've now seen snow and a blizzard for the first time. People, the danger is real ... and very cold."

That got another round of laughter.

Dylan, one of Bexlee's dads, sipped his wine. "You know, Easton and I could go. It's easy for both of us to take time off work. Though we don't know much about the science side of things, Jett knows the science, Katt knows the magic, and we can be drivers. We also own a car that can hold up to seven comfortably."

Georgette narrowed her eyes. "Aren't you an auto tech? Won't your garage be upset if you tell them you want two weeks off?"

Dylan waggled his eyebrows at her. "That's the benefit of returning to work at a place I'd been at for years. I know the owner. If I tell him I need a few weeks, he'll be fine with it. I'm too good for him to risk me not coming back. It's why he was so happy when he saw me walk through his door in September."

Easton glanced at his husband, then sighed. "Dylan's right. I can have someone else do the security at my current location until I get back. They won't mind me taking time off. Don't get me wrong, they won't love it, but the company has such high turnover that when I return, they'll be happy I was really only asking for time off, and not ghosting them."

Bexlee laughed. "You know the term 'ghosting'?"

Easton glared at his daughter. "I'm not that old."

Tamsin felt contentment emanating from the members of her pack. She was annoyed that they were deciding her place in all this, but in the end, she understood. As alpha, she needed to stay in Santa Cruz. When she thought back on the trips she took as a kid, they rarely involved her parents.

Chapter 10 - Sanity ... Check!
Caroline
Wednesday

Caroline looked at her notes. The runes started to blur, and she rubbed her eyes. "I don't know how much more I can do today. I know I asked for longer sessions, but I guess I hadn't really thought this through."

Katt leaned back in the recliner. "Thank the gods. Before we started, I could make my way through these texts, but I wasn't yet fluent in the Power of Seven spells. I know I wrote the one that freed Jett. To me, that's more of a feeling, you know, in here." She rubbed her chest in a small circle with her fist. "But I'm only just barely ahead of you, and reading this for more than an hour makes my head pound."

"I agree. We could do an hour in the morning and another in the afternoon. Or just agree to do some homework ... you know, personal study, between sessions." Caroline gave Katt a wicked grin. The idea of homework over winter break was almost as bad as working over spring break. Somehow, it never was as bad during the summer when the time between sessions was longer.

Katt groaned, then sighed. "As much as I love the idea of homework—" she gave a wry smile, "—next Tuesday, a group of us are driving out to Colorado to see if we can get this think tank to help."

"A what now? Is that safe?" Caroline hated the idea she was being cut out of the process, but if this could be figured out, that was what was important. She clenched her jaw to hide her disappointment from the others.

"I guess it's a werewolf-run group that's been doing research and keeping records on the paranormal for generations."

Caroline narrowed her eyes, anger building within her. This was her project, her research. "Why wasn't I told?"

One of Katt's eyebrows rose. "Probably because it's a werewolf thing."

"Yeah, but I'm the one who's been studying the concoction, doing all the test runs. If this group has a chemist, or is planning on doing any experiments on the tainted tea, they need my research. Or is this group purely theoretical?"

Katt threw her hands out to the side. "No idea. Way above my pay-grade. You'll have to speak to Tamsin about that. I'm going to be dropped off at my parents' house. They said I could go for the drive out, but really, that's it. It sounds like the facility is really for werewolves only."

Caroline nodded, though she was frustrated. They could run as many chemical tests as they wanted but would still fail to find a resolution without knowing the magical side of this problem. "Ah, okay. Well, I'm still going to speak with Tamsin. They'll need my research notes if nothing else."

Once Caroline had packed up her things, she went out to the sidewalk and pulled out her phone. Over the first quarter at UC-Santa Cruz, while working together, she and Tamsin developed a tentative friendship. They'd even exchanged phone numbers. She dialed the alpha as she stepped outside the coven house. She could've driven home, but with nice weather and extra time, she preferred to walk.

"Caroline? What's up?"

"Hi, Tamsin. I was just speaking with Katt—our lessons, you know—and I hear you're taking my mentor away."

Tamsin huffed out a laugh. "Yeah. A group is heading out to Colorado. I was banned from joining them. My pack is awfully opinionated."

Caroline huffed out a laugh. "Admit it, you wouldn't have it any other way."

"Probably not." There was a pause. "Are you just calling to complain about the lessons? That doesn't seem like your style."

"Nope, I'm calling to complain I wasn't invited to join your crew." She hoped Tamsin wouldn't hear her hurt or frustration, but figured the werewolf would pick up on more than she wanted.

There was another silence, longer. It felt tense, even over the phone. "Look, Caroline, this is a werewolf thing. The group invited wolves to a wolf center. I don't think they'd let anyone in who didn't go furry once a month."

"I get that, but I don't think a solution will be found without magic. You need me and the research I've done. I know both traditional magic and everything Katt has been training me. She may be good at archaic magic, but I know this concoction, the traditional magic, as well as the Power of Seven. Admit it, you need me."

After another pause, Tamsin sighed. "Look, I know how frustrating it is to be left behind—"

"It's more than that. I honestly think you need a witch—specifically, me—or your trip will fail. Just ... think about it. Call the people in Colorado. Explain the full extent of what's going on. Try. Please."

Tamsin blew out a gush of breath. "Fine. Give me some time to reach out, and I'll call you back."

Friday

Caroline sat by the beach, studying the runic alphabet. She kept reversing three of the letters, and in a spell, that could be disastrous.

On Thursday, she and Katt had tried one last spell before the pack's Christmas weekend, and the chosen group's eventual trip. It had failed, as always. They were missing something, a key piece.

Caroline picked up the book she'd brought on the Power of Seven, and started at the beginning. She was determined to read the entire thing. *I will master this like I've mastered every other practice I've put my mind to.*

She'd read two and a half pages, a new personal record, when her head began to pound. With a sigh, she leaned back in the beach chair she'd brought, reached down, and grabbed her container of mint tea. Before she could uncap it, her phone rang.

Checking the display, hope and apprehension hit her in equal measures. "Tamsin?"

"Hi, Caroline. Sorry I couldn't get back to you earlier, but getting ahold of Miguel, the alpha of the Colorado pack, is not as easy as it sounds. Apparently, the number I had was for his father's old landline. Anyway, it took some finagling to find him. Once I explained everything to him, he agreed that you joining the party makes sense. So do the others in the group. Oh, and Miguel mentioned our party would need to stay at a hotel. I've made a few calls, and we have a two-bedroom suite with a pullout bed in the living room. It was the best I could get. Is that acceptable?"

Joy bubbled up inside Caroline. She'd won! She was going. "Sounds great. I assume the pullout couch is for me?"

"Unfortunately. The others going are couples. Though, if Jett stays with Katt at her parents', you can have the other room once they're gone."

Saturday

"I can't believe you cleaned!" Sage sounded beyond shocked.

Caroline smiled. She knew her reputation in the coven. "I know how to clean, and I do it regularly. During the school year, it's hard, I'm busy. Now that I have some time off, why not get things tidy?"

"Caroline, I've known you for long enough to know you're a slob."

She threw a pillow at her coven sister, hitting her in her head and messing up her perfectly styled sandy blond hair. Like Cinthia, she wore it held back with a headband that Caroline had just dislodged. "You're such a brat. Now, are you helping me pack or not? I leave with the group on Tuesday, and I don't want to forget anything."

"If I don't help you, does that mean you don't go?"

Caroline rolled her eyes, a practice she'd perfected over the years of teaching teens. "What is it with you?"

Sage shivered as if she were the one to be trapped in a car with wolves. "I don't like werewolves. I don't trust them. I never have."

"Why not? There hasn't been animosity between witches and wolves for longer than you've been alive."

"They're untrustworthy. I don't understand why any of us fraternize with them." Her lip curled in a sneer.

"What about Blake, she's a werewolf as well as a witch."

Sage visibly shuttered. "She should just go back to her own kind and leave us alone. She's completely unnatural. There's never been a wolf-witch hybrid before for a reason."

With a bit of effort, Caroling held a blank face. *I can't believe what I'm hearing, especially from such a young witch.* "Your shortsightedness is holding you back. You know that, right?"

Her hazel eyes bore into Caroline before she chuckled. "Not at all. It's keeping me sane."

"Does Cinthia know how deep your dislike of the werewolves runs?"

"No, and if you'd be so kind as to not tell her? I like this coven and don't want to have to start over."

Caroline eyed Sage. She seemed to mimic Cinthia's style, with long hobo dresses and beaded scarves around her waist. She always appeared to dress as a modern-style hippie.

Caroline shrugged. "I'm leaving town. Your opinions are your own, but in the end, we're all just people with different 'extras.' You do fire magic, I do water magic, and the wolves turn furry. Extras, that's all. No reason to discriminate one specialty over another."

Sage scrunched up her face. "The shifters are shifty; that's why they're called shifters. If they could, they'd do away with us. I mean, you had to ask special permission to go on this mission, right? It's not like they respect us any more than I'm respecting them."

"Whatever. Now, help me pack. I also want a list so that when I head back, all my things come back with me."

Sage searched the room. "Do you even own a winter coat? You know it gets cold there, right? It's December, there's snow."

Chapter 11 - Peace at Work ... Good Time For Research
Mazzy

We wish you a Merry Christmas and a Happy New Year.

Mazzy stood behind a table, listening to the music play. The playlist was long enough that the songs didn't repeat very often.

Most of the people hummed along with the tunes with a smile on their faces. She just endured them. It was her least favorite part of the day.

Ladle in hand, she served peas onto trays of the homeless as they walked by. Last year, she'd served the brownies and received way more appreciation. Being on the veggies was a tougher sell. Then again, for too many people in line, any food was good food.

She smiled at everyone and wished each of them a "Merry Christmas." Many reciprocated the message with small smiles. The younger children broke her heart. She wished she could do more than provide this one paltry meal.

As the morning progressed, her mind wandered. The pack had their annual party at pack house today, but her family also had a tradition of volunteering at a food kitchen on Christmas morning. She loved this more than any of the other seasonal activities she knew about. Her dad always teased that traditions were bullying from ancestors, but she could get behind this one.

She'd called her parents on the drive over to wish them "Happy Holidays." They were a bit more outgoing than her, but not by much. They were on the way to their own volunteering gig.

After what felt like hours on her feet, her shift ended. Circling the room, she smiled at the people eating, wishing them a final "Merry Christmas" before she headed out to her car and collapsed into the driver's seat.

She sat for several minutes, debating her options. The pack would still be celebrating and happy to have her join them, even this late. The thought of going to a party while feeling this drained made her head ache. *It is beyond my already tired state to join such a boisterous group.*

She loved the pack and all its exuberant members, but she needed downtime. In all the years she'd lived in Colorado Springs, she'd never made that final commitment, never moved back into the room they had given her, never dove fully into this pack.

She had her own space and kept herself separate. There wasn't a real reason. In Maine, her family lived with the pack. Her life had always been full of craziness. She'd spent the first few months in Colorado Springs living in pack house, but it always felt wrong, like an outfit that should fit, but was tight in all the wrong spots. She found an apartment a few blocks away, and that was that.

She'd adopted Dennis for companionship, not that a cat was a good substitute for a packmate, but he was something.

She went out for dinner with her pack at least twice a week and of course, there were the people she worked with. That suited her just fine. So many people from the pack had grown up together, this meshed with her need for pack and need for introverted downtime perfectly.

Thankfully, one of Alice's specialties was mental health, and she'd figured it all out and made sure there weren't any hurt feelings.

Sitting up, Mazzy made her decision. There was a mystery, and she needed answers. She didn't care that it was Christmas. It was Monday and that meant work. Being a holiday just meant fewer people around to distract her.

She drove to Sunrise Pharmaceutical, parked, and used her key card to get through locked doors until she reached her lab. *What I need is references to black witches. I need to learn and know more!*

Dropping her bag on one of the lab tables, she headed down the hall to Gus's domain and searched book titles. She would've checked Thomas's, but he was pickier about other people rummaging around in his area.

There were several books on black witches. She needed to find something that related to magic and spells that crossed over to humans. This couldn't be the only time in history they'd been so bold.

After a few minutes of searching, she found one that looked promising. She placed it on

Gus's desk. One wouldn't be enough to keep her busy. Back at the shelves, she scoured the titles. The old adage, you can't judge a book by its cover—or title—wasn't in play today. She didn't want to search through the books, that was Gus's and Thomas's job. Eventually, she found a second book that looked like it had potential. She wrote down the titles and the books' original locations on a piece of paper and left it on Gus's desk, and then she headed back to the lab.

It was time to lose herself in stories of the past.

Chapter 12 - Have You Heard the One About the Witch and The Wolves?
Caroline

One last lap around her small house to make sure everything was turned off, and Caroline was good to go. She couldn't remember the last time her small house was this sparkly clean, but that was her own Christmas gift to herself. She wanted to come home to a place that was clean and shiny. There wasn't even any food in the refrigerator that could spoil; she'd made that mistake once.

Both Cinthia and Sage said they'd stop by and check on her things. She'd told Sage not to bother, because Cinthia lived close enough that one person would be fine. She had a small garden of plants, both inside and out, and if anything started to happen with them, the coven leader had a magic thumb with plants, literally. It was one of her proficiencies.

Pulling out her phone, Caroline checked the itinerary. It would take two days to drive out to Colorado, so they'd get there Wednesday night. The plan was three days working with the crew, but five days *in* Colorado. Friday they were driving back up to Denver to drop off Katt, and possibly Jett. Sunday, New Year's Eve, no one planned on working, though Monday would be a work day. Tuesday, they'd pick Katt back up. Then back to Santa Cruz on Wednesday ... maybe Thursday.

Caroline knew it wasn't enough time to get everything done, but school started the following week, and there was the full moon on that Saturday. Too much to do and not enough time to do it. *Story of my life! Well, maybe the point-person I'm working with will be like the pack here in town and our working relationship will be smooth sailing. We can get the first test done Thursday and, if they have a chemist, the analysis can be done while we're away.*

Through their testing, she and Katt determined letting the solution sit for twelve to twenty-four hours helped increase the potency. She'd retested some of her earlier experiments. Though the results had been the same, the product had been better.

Even with the new system and a full lab at her disposal, Caroline wasn't going to hold her breath. She figured they'd need to backtrack a bit once they reached Colorado Springs. She'd worked with students and been in academia for too long to believe in the fairy tale of smoothly moving forward.

Caroline loaded her purse and duffle on her shoulders and hefted a suitcase. Managing to get herself and everything out the door, she locked up before heading down to the sidewalk to wait for her ride.

A dark gray Honda Odyssey pulled up. The trunk popped open, and she found a place to stuff her two bags. Back by the side door, she saw two men she didn't recognize driving. Katt and Jett sat in the back row. She smiled and waved. "Hi! I take it I get the middle?"

Jett made a displeased face. "The middle has two seats smooshed together. As much as I may like Katt, I like a bit of space, too. You can have the middle, and I'll have a bit of elbow room."

Caroline shut the door behind her and buckled up. She looked at the two men in front, both older, maybe in their fifties. The driver had short brown hair. That was about all she could tell as he pulled away from the curve, checking both the onscreen navigation, and the road ahead.

The other man had blonde hair and blue eyes. He rotated halfway to face her and the others in the car. He had a wide and friendly smile. "Hi, I'm Easton. This is my husband,

Dylan. We're here to make the group look bigger, I'm pretty sure."

She bit back a snort. "Nice to meet you. I'm Caroline. I work with Tamsin at UC-Santa Cruz, as a professor of biology, mainly. I've taught some Intro to Chemistry classes and know some about the other sciences as well. And I want to thank you for allowing me to join you on this trip. I know witches and wolves don't always get along. This being a mixed wagon seems promising to me."

Easton winked. "I thought the same thing."

It didn't take long for them to get onto the open road. Dylan turned on talk radio. Caroline pulled out a book to read. She could hear Katt and Jett in the back talking quietly, but when she checked, they were each doing something on their phones. Games? Movies? Reading? So many options these days.

Once they'd reached a stretch of highway without too many cars, Dylan seemed to relax. "Do you think this is possible?"

Caroline put down her book. "Finding a counter spell or counter remedy to what the black witches have concocted?"

"Yeah. We're only giving ourselves a few days in the lab. From what Bex, um, Bexlee said, the black witches in town took months to perfect what they were doing."

Caroline shook her head. "What now?"

"You haven't been told the full story?"

"I guess not."

Dylan maneuvered around a slow semi-truck. "This really comes from Tory, but we get most of our gossip from our daughter. Tory works as a nurse in the emergency room."

"That, I did know."

"Well, starting last June, maybe it was July, there was a run of homeless people who came in with pulmonary embolisms."

"Wait, what?" Caroline held up a hand. "Give me a second." She closed her eyes and tried to get the puzzle pieces to fit into place. "So, the running theory is, whichever lab created this concoction tested it on the homeless, figuring it would cause less of an uproar. They wanted heart attacks, more natural, but it started out as pulmonary embolisms."

"Right on one, professor. I see we're not working with a half-wit."

"Oh, some days you are, but I'm trying to impress you, so you have me trying to be my best."

Behind her, she heard a snort and assumed it was Jett. The purple haired girl was a bit sassier than Katt.

"So, to recap, we're going to solve in a couple of days that which took the black witches a few months if not years?"

Easton smiled at her, the handsome man winking again. "You got it. And by 'we,' I hope you mean the royal 'you.' Dylan and I are going to crash their pack house and eat all their food."

Caroline barked out a laugh. "Well, that sounds like a plan. That is, of course, if they let me into their secret, werewolf-only lab."

The car got quiet for a moment before Dylan shrugged. "You're here, aren't you? That should prove that you're on the list. VIP access, all the way."

As confident as he sounded, Caroline still wondered. Her stomach clenched at the potential fight ahead of her ... but the war between witches and wolves was over. It would be fine.

Chapter 13 - History of Black Witches
Mazzy

Mazzy sat surrounded by books. After she'd read the two she found on Monday afternoon, she'd gone home and taken notes on what she'd remembered. This morning, she'd given Thomas and Gus a list of things she wanted, including a history of how black witches came into being and when black witches started being a power.

After Gus finished grousing at her for infringing upon his domain, he'd set about fulfilling her request. He had an ability to find reference material where Mazzy was certain there hadn't been anything before. Within thirty minutes, she had a stack to go through. She was pretty sure he thought he was punishing her for looking through his books the day before, but she was excited to start.

Just like wolves and their healing, the black witches of today were a new phenomenon. A few hundred years ago, the black arts were a part of the regular coven repertoire. It wasn't until the witches started using death to boost their spells that they were asked to separate from the rest of their brothers and sisters.

That was another interesting find. Back then, there were more men witches. It was only within the last one hundred and fifty years that the number of men witches had dwindled, almost a direct correlation with the rise of black magic users.

It isn't probable that the two are directly related because men were proficient in all of the magical specialties, but the correlation is interesting. I wonder if any of the coven witches have noticed this. Then there is the period of werewolves almost being hunted to extinction and gaining their powers which was also about that same time. What an intriguing era.

Mazzy picked up another book. Esmeralda Jinx, coven leader extraordinaire, specialized in black magic. When the rest of her coven realized she was using the death of animals around her to aid in her spells, they kindly asked her to leave.

Heh, they kicked her ass to the curb! Get out you bitchy witchy!

Apparently, they didn't see her as an enemy, just a new branch they didn't want to be associated with. She stayed friends with her coven, just separate ... very separate. She moved to a neighboring state, but they continued to send correspondence. See lot M-sixty-eight-D.

Mazzy took note of that but didn't think seeing the correspondence would help in her research. *I just needed a basic understanding of what was going on.*

Within two generations of Esmeralda Jinx, a new history was written for the black witches. See section eleven, book C-forty-eight: Black Witches, the current era. It was on Mazzy's pile.

Ophelia Lynx ushered in a new generation, changing the spells and underlying groundwork of how the black witches worked spells and saw the world. They no longer magicked within the confines of respecting the earth and nature around them, they saw everything as tools to be used in advancing their proficiencies.

As a group, they focused on death and pain. They used the power within plants and their own blood. In extreme cases, the death and pain of animals, and sometimes people, though that was rare, and usually self-governed. A black witch who used life force to empower their spells didn't survive long because of their fellow black witches.

Is all of this malarky that's happening in Santa Cruz about power for spells?

Mazzy took more notes.

Many of the black witches felt their exile from the coven was unfair. Their power source came from natural death, the changing of the seasons, and cycles of death they found without doing harm themselves. *If you found a dying animal and used their end of life to power a spell, are you clever or evil?*

The coven witches countered the argument saying that when the black witches used the turning of the trees to power their spells, the objects they used never came back to life. A tree gone for good. They brought permanent death. That wasn't working in tune with nature, which was anathema to what they believed in.

In the end, the schism that developed after the covens removed the black witches grew to the point of no return. And now, today, the two groups were as divided as witches were from wolves.

Mazzy shook her head. To most wolves she knew, witches and wolves weren't enemies any more. She laid her head on her crossed arms.

She couldn't pinpoint it, but she knew she didn't like them and was glad her alpha didn't expect her to interact with them.

Why do *I have this deep-seated animosity toward the spell-casters?*

95

Chapter 14 - On the Road Again
Caroline

They'd gotten a room with two queen-sized beds and a pullout couch, similar to what they planned on getting once they arrived in Colorado Springs. Caroline wondered about the wisdom of this arrangement as she rolled from the bed with a too-thin mattress. At thirty-six, maybe she was too old for this malarkey.

Her joints creaked as she made her way to the bathroom and turned on the shower. Her shower was quick, though she took an extra couple of minutes to use her magic to turn the hot water into something that pounded down her back and legs. It didn't take long for muscles to relax. Out of the shower, she toweled herself dry, then slipped on her jeans and a sweatshirt. Her long, dark hair would dry soon enough.

She left the small washroom to brush it out, figuring with four other people needing the bathroom, she could get the snags out in front of any mirror.

Everyone else was in and out and ready to go quickly. Being mostly werewolves, they were probably eager to grab something to eat. The hotel offered a free continental breakfast. Caroline made herself some waffles, got a glass of orange juice, and some coffee. She wasn't the fastest eater, but as she made her way through her meal, the three wolves somehow consumed three plates of food each.

She laughed as she selected a banana on her way to the car.

Easton took the first leg of the drive. He sighed. "The food wasn't great, but I like when we can eat our fill, and no one notices how much we consume."

Jett snorted from the back. "*You* like it? Imagine me. I kept up with you two. People see a smallish female and assume all I want is an apple and black coffee. I could starve off people's assumptions."

Katt chuckled and met Caroline's gaze. "Going to one of the pack meals is a hoot. I've never seen so much food placed out on the tables, and by the end, barely any leftovers."

Dylan turned to gaze back at her. "Ah, but the food that our pack chefs prepare is excellent. To not eat it would be a crime."

Katt sighed. "That's true. I can't believe how well some of the wolves cook. Is that how it is with all the packs?"

"Oh, no, dear, not even a little. We're very spoiled with having so many cooks, and not only that, they get along in the kitchen. When we traveled around during the time of the alpha who shall not be named, that was the part we missed the most. That and the camaraderie."

Caroline smiled. "So, is it a requirement to be part of your pack? Make a sample meal first?"

The men up front laughed. Dylan shook his head. "No, there are as many disasters in the kitchen as brilliant cooks. Pack is more about family than food. The food is just the bonus."

Jett leaned forward. "Trust me, I love food, and I hate living alone. I know I pushed back when Tamsin asked me to join the pack, but part of that was because she was my English professor. Part was having been on my own for so long. But inside," she touched her chest, "in here, my wolf howled her acceptance. I knew I couldn't refuse. Not really. Being a wolf means wanting to be in a pack."

Caroline listened, curious. What would it be like? She met Katt's eyes and realized she wasn't the only one. Witches had their coven, but they didn't have the family bond, like the wolves did. Sure, witches got together, but it wasn't a pull. A need. If a witch lived alone, eh, whatever. They didn't need the coven, it was just a nice way to flesh out more complicated spells.

Hearing all this talk of the pack, Caroline thought of her cluttered apartment, empty save for her things, and it occurred to her she was lonely. During the school year, she had her students and colleagues, but during breaks she was alone.

Maybe I should get a dog ... or a cat.

Late that evening, they pulled up to a sprawling building, not unlike the pack house in Santa Cruz. This one was on a plot of private land surrounded by woods. It had three stories and resembled a posh resort.

Caroline and Katt decided to stay in the car. The others just nodded their agreement, uncertain about the reception of witches into a wolf's den. There had been issues in Santa Cruz at one point, but now the pack was more accepting. Here, in Colorado, they were invited guests, and they didn't want to cause any strife.

After about ten minutes, in which the car started to cool dramatically, a tall Latino man came out. His dark eyes danced with his easy smile. He opened the side door. "Now, why did your friends leave you two out here? Are they embarrassed to be seen with two lovely ladies? Come inside, get some hot cocoa, and then I'll kick you out for being heathen witches."

Caroline laughed. "Why, that sounds amazingly welcoming." She held out her hand. "I'm Caroline. Katt is in the back."

"Welcome, Caroline. I'm Miguel, alpha of the pack. Enter in peace." He stepped back, waving his hand towards his home.

A lump formed in her throat at the traditional witch words. "Thank you, Miguel. I enter in peace and hope for nothing but tranquility to you and yours." She bowed her head and walked towards the pack house.

Behind her, she heard Katt say, "Thank you, Miguel. I wish you peace and tranquility."

Inside the Colorado pack house there were only a couple of people aside from the ones she'd traveled with—two men and two women. Miguel waved to them. "I'm sorry, most of my pack is elsewhere. These four work at Sunrise Pharmaceutical Research and Development with me. There is one missing, but you'll meet her tomorrow."

They all sat around the table and enjoyed the hot chocolate. Someone brought out some cookies and they discussed the differences between Colorado Springs and Santa Cruz. After an hour, they left to find the hotel, with directions on where to meet the next morning.

As tired as they were, they all collapsed into beds and couches as soon as they got to their room.

Maybe it would be worth finding someone just to ensure I get a bed next time. Too bad everyone around here is a werewolf.

Chapter 15 - Would We Like to Welcome You?
Mazzy

After reading the history of the black witches and contemplating how she'd go about mixing a concoction that would chemically induce a heart attack, Mazzy set up an experiment to test her hypothesis. She wanted to get it done early Wednesday morning before the people from Santa Cruz arrived. Her results wouldn't precisely mimic what they'd bring, because whatever the black witches created used magic she didn't possess. However, these preliminary trials would provide a starting point to work from.

First, she tested her concoction in a virtual platform. Everything seemed to be in order. Next, she contemplated how to undo, or cure, what she'd created. She consulted with Kaitlyn. The two filled several whiteboards with notes and theories, checking and double-checking their work, formulae, and angles of approach.

The excitement of the chase surged through her. It felt like running through the woods as her wolf, the wind brushing her fur, the aroma of prey in her nose. The chase was on.

Thursday morning, before the Santa Cruz group arrived, the two glared at the boards, trying to figure things out. All the joy from the day before had turned to frustration. Mazzy knew this was a fruitless exercise—they didn't have all the facts they needed—but Kaitlyn was trying to distract her. An hour earlier she'd received a call from Miguel telling her that witches were amongst the Santa Cruz contingent. She'd have to work with witches.

She focused back on the white board. Somewhere in their work was a mistake—just like including witches in her lab was a colossal mistake. Within the equations, something had gone awry. Almost twenty-four hours and two genius minds ... and nothing.

It's like when two wolves chased prey that eluded them, escaped into its den, and they were heading home hungry. Mazzy wanted to howl to the moon in frustration.

"No, Mazzy. I know you're smart, but you're missing a step right here." Kaitlyn tapped the board harder than necessary. "Why do you ignore me when I'm just trying to help you with what you're doing?"

Mazzy sighed and checked over the work again. "Damn it!" She grabbed the eraser and angrily destroyed hours of work. "Okay. If we assume everything to this point is correct, and I don't skip ahead ignoring logic and reason, then where does that leave us?"

Kaitlyn sat back, mouth tight in concentration. She got up and pointed. "What if we bypass here and ..." she trailed off. "Damn, that doesn't work either."

The thought had been nagging at her since she'd read the text. The area had always been werewolf only. Mazzy whipped around. "Why witches?"

Her friend sighed. "Because it was created by magic, you know this. You're going to have to tell someone why you have a phobia against our allies."

"I don't," she answered too quickly. "I just ..." She trailed off. "Look, where I grew up, we saw what happened when black witches destroyed a pack. I was young. I've always known the power they can wield, even over us. It's terrifying. We come from humans. A human can become a werewolf. A human can't just decide they want to join ranks with a witch ... they're different. I don't know."

"When have you been scared of the unknown, my friend?"

She huffed out a breath, wanting to get back to the broken math. Mazzy wanted to bang her head with frustration. She got up to add ... something to the boards. She wasn't sure what. Just then, Miguel knocked on the door frame. She whipped around and snapped, "What?"

He lifted his hands. "Whoa. I just wanted to introduce our guests. Kaitlyn knows them; they came around the pack house last night. But, of course, you weren't there."

She bit back a snarl and forced a smile. The raised eyebrow on the tall, brown-haired man told her her smile wasn't successful. Shaking her head, she took a calming breath and stepped forward. "Hi. I'm Dr. Mazzy Sinclair. And you are?"

"Dylan. I'm sorry to interrupt. My husband, Easton," she saw a shorter man behind him, equally as handsome. "We'll get out of your hair. We just wanted the grand tour. Actually, you can decide whether to have one, two, or three of our party stay. We don't want to overwhelm you."

Mazzy narrowed her eyes. Something didn't feel right. Miguel kept shifting his focus to Kaitlyn like he expected fireworks. *What the hell didn't they tell me?*

"Okay, Dylan. Who else did you bring? You aren't the alpha. I exchanged emails with a 'Tamsin.'"

His smile lit up the room. "No, I'm not an alpha, and thank the gods for that. Tamsin wanted to come, but since we've had some tension back home, we insisted she couldn't leave. There's a black witch uprising in town; not a good time to leave the pack without our fearless leader."

That made sense. It was impressive that their alpha was confident enough in her wolves to trust them with such an important mission. "Okay, but you two aren't scientists?"

"Nope. We had the car and provide good security and pack representation. We brought Jett, a biochem student from UC-Santa Cruz."

Mazzy bristled. "You brought a student? Is she at least a doctoral student?"

A woman who looked to be about fifteen walked up—or was encouraged to move forward by the men behind her. Bleach-blond hair with purple ends. "Sorry. Though I'm old enough to be in my master's or doctoral program, after my pack got destroyed by black witches, I was on my own for years. I only just got enough money together to start college."

"So, you aren't fifteen?"

She laughed. "No, but I get that a lot. I'm actually twenty-six."

Miguel gazed at her. "Wait, you were part of the South Carolina pack?"

Her face fell, then it hardened. "Yeah. I believe I'm the last." Mazzy knew this story, it was the pack that started her animosity towards the witches. Her heart bled for this wolf.

He reached out and grabbed her hand. "I'm sorry. I knew your alpha, he was a good man. I heard about that a few years ago. I didn't know there were any survivors. If I had, I would've looked for you, brought you back here."

A small smile tugged on the side of her mouth. "Thanks. I think things are better now. The witches who took out my pack laid a nasty spell on me. It took the coven in Santa Cruz, and a very clever witch, to figure out how to free me."

Miguel wrapped an arm around her. "I'd like to hear your story."

It felt like Mazzy had been punched in the gut. No witches—not even in name—should be in her lab, though she knew it would be happening soon. She'd been studying them, but that was different. Now they were surrounding them. She could practically smell their herbal scent. Theory, not reality. This was too cordial, and she didn't like it.

The last two members of their group walked in from the hallway, and Mazzy froze, still not ready. She took a step back, sickened by who Miguel allowed into her lab. "No," she whispered, shaking her head. "No."

Miguel cut his eyes to her. "Yes." And there was power behind the single word. Not that she hadn't know, she just needed to get herself over her initial shock. He continued. "People are dying, and if the black witches get a stronghold in Santa Cruz, figure out a way to take out a pack and coven working together in a city that large, what's to stop them from moving east, coming here? We don't have a strong coven in our area. We wouldn't have anyone to help us.

Not to mention, their concoction was created with magic, it needs magic to break it. You can't do it without them."

Witches in my lab? It felt like a pit opened up beneath her feet.

Chapter 16 - My Lab's Bigger Than Your Lab
Caroline

Caroline stepped into the room, immediately distracted by the amazing state-of-the-art lab. She smiled at Kaitlyn, then noticed the beautiful, brunette woman with the smoldering brown eyes. A low snarl kept her from being lost in their lovely depths—currently shooting daggers at her and Katt. As gorgeous as the woman was, she obviously wanted them both gone.

I wonder if we'll be able to work together. Did I make the journey all the way out here only to be kicked out of the lab?

Miguel spoke with forced cheer. "Caroline, Katt, this is Dr. Mazzy Sinclair. You missed out on meeting her last night over hot chocolate."

Caroline looked over to Katt. The younger woman trembled next to her, wide-eyed and looking like prey. In a room full of predators, she knew it wasn't good—they could sense fear, right? Caroline worried that she'd run. Would the pretty scientist run after her? *I knew being a witch in a werewolf-run facility would be an issue.*

With determination, Caroline stepped forward. "Your lab, though a bit small, is lovely." The lab wasn't small at all, she just needed to distract the fire in that woman's eye away from Katt. She waved at the board. "Nice job with the equations, though you're missing an alpha in the third row, and it would work better if you tweaked the formulae on that board." She pointed to the last board. "It would make it possible for you to finish what you started. You're moving your chemistry towards a biological leaning, and that's your problem. I mean, it would come to a solution ... eventually. But you need to understand the biology first."

She turned to face Dr. Sinclair. "Getting to the point of our twenty-hour drive to invade your lab, I've worked on countering the black witch concoction, using five trials to be exact, and I have copious notes. I'm here to work with you, to complement the work you've done. Kick me out if you want, but the fact is, you'll never solve this problem without a witch." She smirked, folding her arms over her chest.

Mazzy looked ready to explode. "My lab is small? How dare you belittle our facility." Behind the cantankerous woman, Kaitlyn's eyes were large, and it looked like she tried to signal Caroline against antagonizing Dr. Sinclair, but Caroline worked at a university and knew about big egos.

Caroline shrugged. "It's quaint. I mean, don't get me wrong, I've worked in smaller places, but this will do." She thought she heard the people behind her shuffling to get into better positions in case Dr. Sinclair was pushed too far. They just had to trust her. She knew scientists.

The wolf narrowed her eyes. "And where do you work?"

"At a university. My opinion of labs may be skewed by the fact that my lab needs to be big enough for a gaggle of teens."

One of Dr. Sinclair's eyebrows rose. "Gaggle? Like geese?"

"Yep, both are noisy and are dangerous if not monitored closely."

The other woman's face twitched. "Okay, that's funny." A small smile flashed on her face. "Okay, fine. You can read our boards, find mistakes, and have research for us to review. I won't kick you out of my lab ... not yet." She swiveled to her alpha. "But only the one. No students. We do real work here, no training."

Kaitlyn coughed softly. "*Our* lab. You may be good at what you do, but so am I."

"Fine, our lab. But I stand by what I said, no students." She sounded offended, but Caroline wasn't about to antagonize her more.

She turned to Caroline. "Okay, we have work to do, and from what I understand, you lot are out of town tomorrow. Let's start over. I'm Dr. Mazzy Sinclair, but you can call me Mazzy."

Caroline smiled wide. "I'm Dr. Caroline Dobbs, and you can call me Caroline. Nice to meet you. If you're ready, I'd love to get started. Tomorrow we need to get another book on spell-casting from Katt's family up in Denver. Her parents were unavailable when we drove through, so we had to wait until Friday. We'll return before bedtime and be back here on Saturday."

"So, Katt will be staying with her parents?" Mazzy sounded hopeful.

"Yes. She came to help with a specific type of magic that she knows better than perhaps any witch I know ... and to see her parents."

Katt shook her head. "You're getting to be as good as I am with the Power of Seven. I'm a bit more fluid with the ancient stuff, but you can muddle through it well enough to make it work. And I'm only a phone call away."

She's downplaying her abilities because she just wants to go home. She misses her parents, and I don't blame her.

Caroline smiled at her warmly. "I don't know if that's true, but you're right, I can always call you if I need your expertise. Denver isn't that far."

Mazzy seemed to relax. "Okay, so no arguments on one addition to the lab. I think I can handle that better than two or three. But you're a witch." She took a deep breath, then rubbed her nose. "I guess I'll have to get used to that, as well. At least you know some science."

Caroline knew a compliment when she heard one, and that wasn't one. She smirked; this was like working with her students. She turned to Dylan and Easton. "I think you can leave me here. She probably won't eat me. I'll call when I need a ride home. Go, enjoy the other wolves. Be ambassadors from the West."

The men smiled. "Yes, ma'am!"

Jett's brow furrowed. "Are you sure? Katt and I could help for the day. You know our skills."

Before Caroline could open her mouth, Mazzy stepped closer. "No, we're fine. She can call if we need more helpers." She shooed with her hands. "One witch in my lab is enough. Go. Now."

As they walked out, Caroline wondered what she'd gotten herself into and why she was so determined to be there.

Chapter 17 - I'm A Scientist, Not a Diplomat
Mazzy

With a sense of dread, Mazzy watched her alpha lead the three wolves and the one younger witch out of her lab. That left Caroline. The witch was beauty personified, with long dark hair, nearly black, and dark eyes. When she had walked into the lab, the woman had practically glided, and Mazzy's heart had skipped a beat before the scent hit her, and she recognized her for what she was.

Both Miguel and Kaitlyn seemed to accept a witch in the midst of top-secret wolf research as nothing to sweat about, but Mazzy knew something fundamental had changed, and she didn't like it. This was wolf territory. How could they allow it to be invaded by the enemy?

She needed a moment to gather her thoughts. "You said something about a power? A new magic system?"

"Old," Caroline corrected. "Antiquated, it's so old. Power of Seven. It's something that witches talk about, but I've never heard of anyone using, until Katt showed up. Not only did she bring it to our coven, she started teaching anyone who wanted to learn. I'm convinced it's the only way to break through the black magic that's in the concoction."

Mazzy realized she was getting caught up in Caroline's story. *I need to get away before she puts some witchy spell on me. Fuck!* "Why don't you and Kaitlyn work on the boards while

I go speak with Thomas and Gus in the archives? We may have something on this magic system; stranger things have happened. When I get back, I'd like to start studying the concoction and look over your notes."

The modelesque witch took a moment before she nodded. "Okay, sounds like a plan." She turned to Kaitlyn and her smile brightened the room. Mazzy almost forgot to breathe.

She tore herself from the lab. *Do not get infatuated with a witch. I know she isn't the enemy anymore, but she is a witch and I'm a werewolf. Moreover, she's a witch who lives in Santa Cruz. What the hell is wrong with me?*

She stomped into Gus's office, mumbling under her breath.

"I see you've met the crew from California." His eyes danced with amusement.

She rolled her eyes. "Not you, too. They brought witches, Gus, witches! There's one in my lab right now." She threw her hands in the air as she snarled.

"Caroline? She seems like she knows a thing or two about what's going on. She's also funny." He winked with a smile.

A growl reverberated from her gut, and he laughed. "Enamored, I see. So, why are you here if there's an intruder in the lab? Shouldn't you be keeping a watch over her, make sure she doesn't steal the glassware, or something?"

She tried to hold her glare, but his amusement filled the room, and she finally chuckled. "She mentioned something about a power, um, the power of seven?"

He swung around in his seat and rolled over to a computer. He picked up his phone and called Thomas, filling him in on her request. She could hear both sides of the conversation as they both typed away.

Gus got up and found an old leather-bound book with a scuffed cover. "The only thing I'm finding is referenced in this one. It isn't one of the magic books, so I'm guessing it won't be very useful."

Mazzy took the heavy beast of a book. It thrilled her to read such an old book, but she feared harming it. She skimmed until she found the section.

The Power of Seven, a powerful magical art, was replaced by proficiencies in the late sixteen hundreds. There are several factors for the shift from the old to the new magical systems. The main one being the complexity of the runes, which are the backbone of the Power of Seven. At the time, witches were being hunted, and the practice of teaching the runistic arts took a toll on the practitioners. The time to master the arts is three to fourfold that of mastering a single proficiency, such as fire or water.

When the witches realized they could tap into different aspects of the elements and energy around them, they focused on that. Within a few generations, the Power of Seven became more myth than reality.

Though a few witches today possess knowledge of this archaic artform, for most, the Power of Seven is a cautionary tale told to entice the young to study and not forget, lest their current system go the way of the old.

Mazzy handed the book back to Gus with a sigh. "This won't help the witch. It's an interesting background, but it isn't practical."

From the phone sitting on the desk, Thomas's voice came through clearly, though he was obviously away from his phone like they were. "I don't have anything here. I've done a few checks. I think what you found is all we have."

"Well, fuck. Thanks." Mazzy sighed. So much for their all-knowing research team.

Gus pushed the book back into Mazzy's hands. "Are you sure you don't want to share this with Caroline? A bit of a peace offering?"

"Why would I need a peace offering?"

"Oh, I don't know. I'm just guessing you haven't been completely hospitable."

She snarled again and snatched the book from him. "Fine, I'll show the witch the damn book."

"You do know she has a name."

"Whatever!"

Back in the lab, the whiteboards had changed a bit. An elegance met her. It made her blood boil. She tossed the book at the witch. "That can't leave the lab."

Caroline's brow rose as she grunted with the impact. "Okay. Thanks?"

"Whatever," Mazzy mumbled, hopefully too softly for human and therefore the witch's ears to catch. She knew she was being childish, but she needed time to care.

She saw papers laid out on a workbench. Heading over, she observed each of the experiments written up in complete duplicatable details and precision notes. She read from left to right, getting lost in the progression of the witch's logic.

She hated to admit that she was impressed by what she read. The last two reports utilized this "Power of Seven." When she finished, she looked up to see the other woman sitting at her unused desk reading the book she'd tossed her.

"So, you've set up these experiments and used magic each time. What's missing?"

The witch reached into her bag and found a bookmark. Mazzy's brows rose at the sight of an actual bookmark. She carefully shut the book and placed it on the desk. *Gus would be in love with the care she took.*

She turned to Mazzy and smiled. "Did anyone tell you that werewolves are immune to this?"

Mazzy was dumbfounded. Kaitlyn's expression mirrored her own. Mazzy stared at the witch. "What?" They'd debated the possibility, then threw it out. After over a century, the black witches must have perfected a way to infect even wolves. They were parasites, worse than the coven witches.

"Yep," Caroline's eyebrows wiggled. "The concoction doesn't affect wolves. One of the pack wolves who works as a police officer, her partner was poisoned, it's how we got the concoction. To save him, she bit him ... turned him. It was a big thing since they couldn't ask him first."

Mazzy was disgusted at the hubris of changing someone without their consent or knowledge. She saw her own shock on Kaitlyn's face, a sneer forming with her growl.

A small snarl escaped Kaitlyn. "A man was changed without consent?"

The witch shrugged. "I'm not a werewolf and don't know your customs. I do know that there was a discussion beforehand and the officer said she knew he'd accept if asked. Apparently, they'd had enough conversations that were close to the topic."

"You know a lot for not being Pack." Mazzy snapped, taking her ire out on the innocent witch—if a witch could be considered innocent.

"I do. The coven and pack are friends in my city. I talk with Jett and Katt often, and they got the story from Cyrus, the one who was changed. Jett has even helped with some of his training. He's okay with me knowing his story. If he wasn't, then I wouldn't know about it. I also work at the same college as the werewolf alpha, and we have lunch together about once a week."

Mazzy rubbed her face. "You lot are different from anything I'm used to."

"Do you know many witches?"

Mazzy shivered. "Gods above, no!"

"Can we move on to the concoction?" the witch asked, amusement in her voice. "We only have a few days, and I want to make sure we actually accomplish something."

As much as Mazzy didn't like being led in her own lab, she had to agree. The three of them got to work.

Chapter 18 - Mind Over Matter
Caroline

The couch was awful. It was a disaster. Caroline tried to sit up gracefully, but every muscle in her body complained when she tried to move. She wondered if she'd ever get a good night's sleep again. *Focus on the good. Tonight, you can sleep in a real bed. Katt and Jett are staying with Katt's parents.*

She tried to bite back her groan as she pushed herself up, but failed. At least it was soft. No one but her would know.

"You okay out there? Should I send help?" There was laughter in Dylan's voice. Jerk!

"I'm fine. Nothing to see here." She slumped down before managing to get herself to her feet.

Caroline hobbled into the bathroom, shut the door, and set the shower to as hot as she could handle without burning her skin off. She stepped in and let the pressure massage her body. The heat seeped in, and she felt herself relax. *I should sleep in here. It may be better. Even if the others use the facilities, I could just slide the shower curtain shut.*

She snorted at her own goofy thoughts.

She used a bit of magic and created a whirlwind of water to envelop her body until every inch of her was covered with the spinning warmth. Closing her eyes, she squeezed her fingers, and the warm water tightened around her, like a pulsating massage blanket.

She sighed and kept up the pressure for a few minutes before releasing her hold. It used a lot of her power, but her body sang with the feeling of contentment once it was done.

Feeling human—or as human as she could, with a bed like that—she stepped from the tub, dried off, and slipped on her clothes. As she had done the day before, she finished drying her hair and getting prepared outside of the bathroom, letting the others have time in the single most popular room. She'd taken too much time letting the water soothe away her aches and pains. When she opened the door, she saw the others loitering around near the door. She smiled weakly before skittering away.

Caroline folded up the evil hide-away bed and brought out some books to study the runes while the others prepared for the day. She wanted to make sure she got through some of the tricky material while Katt was still around to help.

Once everyone was ready, they headed down for the hotel complimentary breakfast. Caroline marveled once again at the amount the wolves could eat. She'd always had a small appetite. Sometimes she wished she could eat more, if only to enjoy trying more variety at places with buffets. She knew, in theory, that werewolves burned more energy, but spending this much time with them delighted her. It was nice getting a chance to see them as people and learn more about another group of paranormals.

Easton, Dylan, and Jett went for their third plates as Katt, next to her, scoffed. "I don't know how they all stay so fit. They're all so pretty, too. If it didn't mean I'd lose my magic, I might consider doing what Mildred did, just so I could eat all the food."

Caroline shook her head. "Not me. I mean, don't get me wrong. If I were in Cyrus's position, then yeah—life over death. Well, maybe." Caroline scrunched up her face. "Okay, yes. But beyond that, I'd choose to keep my magic."

Katt sipped her coffee. "Yeah. In the end, I agree. I can't imagine not having the power flowing through me. There are times I reach for my power and don't even realize I'm doing it.

If I lost my ability to touch the earth ..." She shivered. "Okay, you win. Staying a witch, it is!"

After eating, they piled into the car and put Katt's address into the GPS. Katt visibly relaxed as she watched the scenery go by. Every now and again, she pointed out something and told a quick anecdote about what she'd done there with family or friends. She was home and Caroline could hear the stress leaving her body as she got closer and closer to her family. She spoke faster and the happiness was obvious.

"And over there, in that building, Mom told me that she and Dad were getting married. She also told me, if I wanted, that he'd adopt me."

From the front, Dylan asked, "How old were you?"

"Six. It was an amazing day. I'll never forget it."

Facing sideways, Caroline saw Jett's eyebrow raised in question.

Katt smiled. "He'd been 'Dad' to me for so long, the idea of making it official seemed obvious, even at such a young age. I remember being so excited that I got chills. I said, 'Yes, yes yes!' Then I put my arms around him for a big hug. He swung me around and my feet flew out. It's one of those happy memories that will stick with me." Her head jerked towards the window. "Oh! Turn here, it's faster."

Easton turned.

Dylan's head swung back and forth. "But, wait, we aren't supposed to turn for another mile and a half."

Katt huffed out air in a laugh. "Trust me. In three blocks, turn left, and the GPS should catch up with us."

Just as predicted, the ETA dropped by a few minutes. When they finally parked, Caroline was thrilled to get out and stretch. In a few days, she'd spend two more days locked up in that beast of a box... with the beasts. But for now, she wanted to move her muscles. A small moan of appreciation escaped her.

Behind her Easton chuckled. "You sound part wolf, Caroline. We hate being cooped up, too. Being able to move around is what we live for."

Dylan's voice dropped to a stage whisper. "It isn't all we live for, dear."

They approached Katt's family's front door to the sound of chirping birds and Easton's laughter.

Katt opened the door and didn't even get a step in before her mom engulfed her in a hug. "Katt, love, you made it!"

Caroline gaped at the woman. People always told mothers and daughters that they could be sisters, but in this case, the resemblance was uncanny. She remembered Katt telling them her mom was young when Katt was born, but her mom looked Caroline's age. She had long dark hair, like Katt, and as the two separated, she saw vivid blue eyes. The woman was stunning.

She gazed at the group and audibly gulped. "So, you're all ... um ..."

As Caroline stepped forward, Dylan and Easton eased back. "Hi, Mrs. Anton, I'm Caroline Dobbs. I was your daughter's chemistry professor this past quarter. I'm ... like the two of you."

A glance to her left and right told her there were no neighbors with their heads in the windows, but she wasn't sure if any of them could overhear the conversation. "We came with Jett, who I'm sure you've heard all about, and these are our drivers, Dylan and Easton."

Mrs. Anton nodded quickly. "Yes, right. Why don't you all come in? We have refreshments in the dining room. Is a charcuterie board good? Cheese and crackers? Some sausage and wine?"

Behind her, Caroline heard the moans of delight from her travel companions.

Katt bobbed her head. "That's perfect, Mom."

She led them all through a tight hallway, past a cozy living room, and into a nice dining room with a table that would fit eight comfortably. It had a few pictures on the wall and a fancy chandelier. Besides what Katt's mom had mentioned, a plate filled with fruit and another featuring pastries sat on the center of the table. It all looked delicious.

Katt's dad came in from the living room. He was tall and a bit thick around the middle.

His brown hair was thinning, but his eyes, like the rest of the family, showed happy humor. He and Katt hugged, and he kissed the top of her head.

"I missed you, bug."

"I missed you, too, Dad."

He turned to the group. "Hi, I'm Mitchel."

They each introduced themselves. Katt's mom insisted on being called Violet.

They all sat and spent a few minutes eating. Katt and her parents talked about college and the drive. The others gave them a few minutes to catch up.

Then Caroline cleared her throat. "The three of us would like to give you time together. We're going to head back to Colorado Springs for a few days, but before we leave, I was hoping I could help release some of your younger memories."

Violet blanched. "I don't know. I've lived this long as I am. What does it matter?"

Katt placed a hand on her mom's arm. "Please, Mom. For me? I'd like to know more about your past—our past. This is one of her proficiencies. I told you about your family's coven and that they were attacked by black witches. Something similar is happening back home."

"This is your home, Katt." A fire of determination burned behind Violet's eyes.

"I know, but I meant Santa Cruz."

Violet's face hardened. "I'm not sure, love. I can't see how that can help you figure anything out."

Jett shut her eyes. "You know, when your daughter freed my mind, I got memories of my parents I never thought I'd get back. They are some of the most precious things I now have. I wouldn't give them up for anything."

She didn't shrink when she opened her eyes and saw everyone staring at her.

Finally, Violet sighed. "I don't like this. First werewolves, then a coven witch, and now you want me to trust her to mess with my mind? You're asking for a lot, Katt."

"Please, Mom."

She sighed. "Fine, but I think this is a colossal waste of time."

In the living room, they set up two chairs so that Caroline could easily place her hands on Violet's temples. They both closed their eyes and breathed deeply.

Taking in a deep breath, Caroline let her power flow out, forming a mental bridge between her and Violet.

Chapter 19 - Trial and Error
Mazzy

"Can you believe the mess she left in my lab?"

"Our lab." Kaitlyn sighed.

"Just look at this place. Who does she think she is?" Mazzy continued, stomping around, cleaning, and ignoring her partner.

"A brilliant scientist who helped progress our research by days if not weeks?" Kaitlyn raised an eyebrow in challenge.

Mazzy whipped around. "Whose side are you on?"

"I'm not 'on' anyone's side, Mazzy, I just want to get this job figured out, and you're focusing on trivial matters." She sounded exasperated, which wasn't unusual in their interactions.

"The state of the lab isn't trivial."

Kaitlyn sat on one of the stools. "Mazzy, the lab isn't that bad. You're just a bit picky. Caroline helped us run the first test of the concoction and in an hour we can test it again."

"It'll fail," Mazzy snapped. She knew she sounded petulant, but she didn't care. She crossed her arms and glared at the counter-concoction that she knew wouldn't work.

"Of course it'll fail. It's a baseline. The point is to give us information. If we thought it would succeed, then we wouldn't test it without Caroline here."

That silly sexy witch who has decided she can just come in and judge my lab, as if she has any right. Godsdamnit! Not sexy, just a scientist who happens to be a witch. Mazzy circled the lab. She had too much energy to sit and wait.

"Don't you have one of the research books you can read? I have my own project to work on while we wait, and your pacing doesn't help," Kaitlyn snarled.

Pausing, Mazzy shook out her hands and gazed at the stack of books and research papers. "Yeah, fine. I can do a bit of reading. Some of what I've learned has helped. More has just been interesting."

"Good, go, stop being a menace."

She smiled. *Gods above, I'm acting like Dennis!* Flopping down on the couch along the side of the lab, she picked up a scientific paper that crossed over between the topic of her research studies and the current challenge. *Black Witches and Werewolves: A History.*

In the beginning, Esmeralda Jinx walked away from the covens, taking the black witches with her. After a few generations, Ophelia Lynx

created a new witch paradigm, reinventing them into what is seen today. Before her push to completely redefine black witchcraft, there was hope that black witches may one day rejoin their sisters.

However, once the black witches fully embraced utilizing pain and death to boost their spells, rejoining the covens was no longer an option.

The divide grew, and within a few generations, the two groups went from family to friends, from respect, to enemies. At the time of the writing of this paper, black witches and coven witches do not get along.

It did not take long for the black witches to learn spells to harm their sister coven witches. One on one, it is even money that the black witch will win the battle. They do not play fair. Their magic messes with the mind of humans and witches alike.

There are reports that the black witches have sought out the coven witches to take over their locations, annihilating them to tap into the ley lines they built their coven homes over.

Once the black witches figured out how to take down a coven, (see Black Witches and Their War on Covens: A History) They moved on to werewolves.

At first, the theory was the shift centered on proximity. Werewolf packs and witch covens often dwelled close by to one another; the power of the ley lines help both groups. After a battle with a black witch in which a werewolf gained access to papers found at the black witch's home, a new conclusion came to light. (See Notes and Paper: The Mad Ramblings, Inner Thoughts, and Motivations of a Black Witch.)

The heart of the issue seems to have started with Ophelia Lynx. For years, she encouraged the black witches to seek out werewolves, hoping to gain the secret of werewolf healing. Their strategies have evolved, starting with killing and eventually moving to capture. The challenge with capture is it involves facing wolves in battle.

Many black witches were lost in these battles. In a face-to-face altercation, the wolf wins. It takes a group of three or more black witches to ensure a single spell will lay successfully on a wolf, and then it only works if the wolf is not prepared.

Newer reports state that the black witches decided to test what they would need to do to control wolves as well as gain some of their power. They spent the better part of the next century trying to figure out how to enspell a werewolf. Some reports show they have mastered casting a long term spell on one wolf, but have yet to learn a broad spell that will affect more than one at a time. They have lost more of their black witch brothers and sisters than they have gained information. Unfortunately, a few werewolf packs were lost in the silent war.

Despite years of work and diligence, at the time of the writing of this paper, no black witch group has figured out how to enspell more than a single werewolf.

Chapter 20 - Origins
Caroline

Violet's mind had a sticky web over it, but with Caroline's magic, and a bit of what she'd learned from Katt and the Power of Seven, getting down to her memories felt like sliding into a dream.

Where did everyone go? Mom said she'd meet me in the kitchen, and I'd get a push-pop before going to the park.

Violet shivered at how quiet the house felt. She'd spent an hour in her room, just as instructed. She had a small reading area in her closet—it was the only quiet place in the coven house—and she'd read about frogs. Now that she'd finished her reading, she was ready for her treat! But where was everyone? She didn't like it when she couldn't find her parents or any of the other coven witches.

What's that? Whose voices are those? I don't recognize them. I know everyone who comes to coven house.

Mom always told her to hide if she was afraid. As long as she came when called by someone she knew, being scared wasn't bad. She slid into the crawlspace between the pantry and the broom closet. It was just her size and one of her favorite hiding places to spy on the adults.

"Did you get them all?" A tall woman with red hair sauntered into the kitchen.

Who is that?

"Yep," a shorter, dark-haired woman said. "One couple for testing, the rest are dead. We can bring that wolf here for testing."

Violet didn't recognize either of the women. Fear chilled her.

The red-haired woman sat at the table with the dark-haired woman. "There has to be a way. Why can't we control them? They're just mutts, all of them."

The dark-haired woman shook her head. "The last wolf we tested on died. I don't know what you're trying to do here, Jackie."

Jackie's a silly name for the red-haired girl. She should be called Cinnamon or Cherry. It'd match her hair better. And the other woman should be called Chocolate. Cherry and Chocolate! Violet had to cover her mouth to not laugh out loud. She was nervous but also amused. She wondering why they were talking about wolves and dying, especially at a witch's home.

Cherry scrunched up her face at Chocolate. "There has to be a way we can affect all the wolves at one time. The idea they're immune to us is insane. We control the animals, not the other way around."

Chocolate banged her hands on the table, hard. All the muscles in Violet's body tensed. Chocolate sneered. "You do know that this is a pipe dream that the black witches have been spouting off for years, right? Ever since Ophelia Lynx made it a founding goal. But it'll never happen. We should find a place to build up our numbers, not run around focusing on coven witches and wolves. It's a deadly waste of time."

A dark look passed over Cherry's face and a shiver ran down Violet's back. "I could cast a lot of spells using you. Don't mess with me."

"Fine. Where do you want to do this?"

"In here. We'll tie the wolf to a chair. Maybe it's something in their blood."

All their words made Violet cold inside. She didn't really understand them, but she knew they were wrong. She wondered where Mom and Dad were and why these people were in a coven house speaking like this.

They dragged a man in. He was fit, with brown curls. He wasn't wearing a shirt or pants, and that made Violet's cheeks heat up. *Why don't they let him put on clothes? He'll get cold only wearing undies. They're really mean!*

They tied him to a chair, and the rope was too tight. She could see his skin turn red. Violet whimpered as she trembled.

All three adults turned to face her. Cherry stomped over and yanked her out of her hiding spot by her shoulder. "Ouch!" she cried out. "Why are you here? You don't belong in our house. Where's my mom? Where's my dad?"

Cherry turned to Chocolate. "Go get that couple locked up in the basement, the one we're testing the curse on. I have an idea." Her gaze dropped to Violet. "A new use for them."

A shiver ran down Violet's back. *Who are they hurting? Are they going to curse me, too?*

A few minutes later, one of Mom's friends, Lydia, was dragged in, with her husband Clifford. They were two of Violet's usual babysitters.

Cherry sneered at them. "Take the girl away, to a different state. Do not join a coven.

Do not speak to anyone about any of this. If you do, we'll know, and we'll kill you all. This is a one-time offer for survival."

Clifford's eyes narrowed. "You cursed us. We won't survive the year."

A smile played across the woman's face. "Figure it out."

Cherry pulled out a knife and cut a line in the tied up man's thigh. He didn't make a sound, but the woman said some words. It felt like a blanket was put over Violet's mind, and everything went dark.

Chapter 21 - Blood to Blood
Mazzy

Saturday morning, Mazzy and Caroline agreed to meet up in the lab to work. Kaitlyn decided to take the weekend as well as New Year's Day off, but said to call her if they came up with anything or needed her brilliance. She had plans before the Santa Cruz contingent came, and she wasn't about to drop them for the early stage tests.

When Mazzy got to the center, Caroline waited outside the door. No one had given her access. Though dressed in a winter coat, hat, scarf, and boots, she looked miserably cold. A small smirk played across Mazzy's face. *The witch may be able to get into my lab, but only with my permission.*

"Good morning, w—Caroline." Mazzy corrected herself just in time.

"Morning, Mazzy."

She led the other woman through the maze of halls until they got to the lab. They didn't speak. Caroline rubbed her hands together the whole time, apparently trying to warm up. When they got to the lab, she looked around. "You don't happen to have a way to make coffee, do you? I'll even cook."

Mazzy shrugged as she went to look over the lab notes from the day before, pointing towards the small kitchen.

From the corner of her eye, she watched as Caroline put down her bag and headed over to start a pot of coffee. Mazzy appreciated her perfect curves from the back as she waited for the machine to finish brewing. *Stop, she's a witch and, while here, a colleague. Not someone to lose your mind over!*

Once Caroling had a cup of coffee, she curled her hands around the mug. *Gah! It isn't that cold!* She finally made it over to the workbench. "So, what did I miss yesterday?"

"What we set up on Friday failed."

"Fair, fair. Details?"

Mazzy stiffened. "You can read the notes."

"Excellent. Lab notes not written by students—my heart may not survive!" She walked over and began reading, a huge smile on her face. "Okay, this looks good. Wait, this is interesting."

Mazzy snatched her notes back. "I didn't mean for you to read that last part." She'd added a bit about what she'd learned about the black witches and wolves.

Caroline shook her head. "Why not? Let me tell you about my day yesterday."

With effort, Mazzy stopped herself from rolling her eyes. *Why would I care about how she wasted time when we had real things to accomplish?* "I'm not that interested. We're here for a job. Visiting a witch in Denver doesn't seem helpful to our cause."

"You'd be surprised." Caroline took a deep breath. "Look, I know you don't like me. You have a thing against witches."

"Who told you that?" Mazzy didn't mean to snap, but the idea that her pack spoke about her behind her back hurt.

"No one," Caroline laughed. "You've made it plain as day since I walked in the lab. Your pack is pleasant and tries to hide your distaste. You're lucky to have them."

Mazzy rolled her eyes. "Whatever. It isn't like they have to protect me."

"Okay, the point is, the woman we visited yesterday was the only surviving coven witch of a black witch attack some thirty-five-ish years ago. She witnessed the start of a werewolf ... well, I don't know what. It was the memories of a four-year old. But there was something there. The black witches, I guess, have been testing on your people, trying to find some holy grail, ever since some founding black witch of the past set them on the trail."

With a wave of her hands. Mazzy indicated her books. "It's all in there. I've been studying black witches. The books can't leave the lab, but you're welcome to do some light reading."

"Do you think we need to somehow incorporate wolf healing into our counter-concoction? Is that a thing?" Caroline had her nose in the notes, looking over the previous tests failures and how they compared to her failures before arriving in Colorado.

Mazzy realized she couldn't stay irate forever; it took too much energy. For the next few days, she'd treat Caroline like any other scientist. Try to forget the fact that she was a witch. Ignore the stench ... no, the earthy scent didn't smell bad, it was just the association she'd always made. She'd ignore the herbal smell and focus on the work. "It's the basis of the research I was doing before the Pacific Pack alpha contacted me. I'm not sure if werewolf healing *can* be used to help non-wolves, but I think you're right that we need to think about it. Where do you want to start?"

"I think the obvious is blood. I don't know what in your blood makes you *you*, but have you tried a drop in a healing solution before?"

Face hard, Mazzy shook her head. "It isn't that simple."

Caroline shrugged. "Then what's your great idea?"

Rubbing her face, Mazzy sagged against a table. "Fine, we'll try it your way. Let's set up a series of twelve tests. We'll utilize the next step in the chemical compound you've been synthesizing. Your start is good, but it can go farther, here and here." Mazzy tapped the last page of lab notes Caroline had brought. "Your chemistry needs work." She tried to keep her voice light, the way she would've spoken to Gus or Thomas.

She went over to a whiteboard and wiped it down. "Next, I want to create a set of four solutions that have a variation of higher concentrations of blood that don't utilize magic, four that use the basic magic you've been using from the start, and the final four that try the Power of Seven. How does that sound?"

Across the room, Mazzy saw a wide smile on Caroline's face. "Oh! This is going to be fun. Can you start on the chemistry side while I work on the spells? Katt gave me three Power of Seven books to bring along after we dropped her off yesterday. I was up way too late last night reconfiguring a spell I think will work better. I still need to work on the base magic spell, though."

Mazzy nodded and they both got to work.

Once they had everything set up, Mazzy watched as Caroline ran the tests. She had two versions of magic to set and four of each to chant out. After eight mixtures, the witch almost collapsed. Mazzy wrapped an arm around her and helped her to the couch. "Are you okay?"

"Yeah. These spells look small, but they carry a big punch. I just ... dizzy."

"Do you need anything? We've been working for hours. How about I grab some food? What do you like?"

"Hmm." She groaned. "Anything sounds amazing. My coven leader always yells at me for magicking without proper sustenance."

"Wait, you need extra calories for this much magic? Like our shifts? And you didn't tell me? For fuck's sake, Caroline. The mixtures need to wait until tomorrow. Let's go. I assume you were dropped off. Food first, then I'll drive you to the pack house."

"Hotel."

"What?"

"Witch. We were told we needed a hotel to keep the wolves less agitated."

"Ah. Makes sense. Welcome, but not *that* welcome. Glad to know I'm not the only one in the pack who's kept you at arm's length." She shook her head. "Okay, then, let's go."

They had Chinese food. Over the meal, like at the lab, Mazzy was determined to treat Caroline as a person, a colleague, and not a hated witch. The intense smells of the food helped cover the herbal scent.

Mazzy learned about Caroline's college and what type of professor she was. Mazzy told her a bit about her volunteer work. The meal was surprisingly pleasant.

Chapter 22 - Taming the Wild Beast ... Or Not
Caroline

The bed in the hotel was soft as a cloud. After a couple days on couches, Caroline wanted to purr. She stretched and rolled over, luxuriating in the large bed.

It was New Year's Eve. The pack had a celebration and they'd invited her, Dylan, and Easton, but Caroline didn't want to go. She knew everyone would be happier ringing in the new year without a witch there. Miguel had tried to convince her to come, but she had been steadfast in her decision.

If she were back in Santa Cruz, she'd order pizza, have some locally brewed beer, and watch a movie. She may have hung out with Cinthia, but more likely she'd just stay home alone. She wasn't into partying with big crowds. In reality, she was an introvert who appeared to the world like an extrovert. After the trip and constantly being surrounded by others, she needed some time alone to recharge.

Once up and ready to face the day, she met the men in the living room.

"What do you say we hit a buffet for breakfast, get something more than what's offered here?" Easton smiled wide. "I know we've spent most of the last several days traveling, and then you were in the lab all day yesterday. We need a good brunch."

"That sounds delightful. But, afterward, can you drop me off at the lab? I really want to get the work done while I'm here." She sat on the couch and put on her shoes.

"Really?" Dylan came out of the bathroom, head tilted. "Why work? It's a Sunday and a holiday. There's a party tonight."

She slumped back. "I know, but I think everyone will be happier with me in the lab ... including me. Don't worry. If I were back home, then I'd probably be alone as well. It's all good."

Dylan's face scrunched up before he nodded in agreement. "If you're sure, I won't push. I think everyone would welcome you. From our time with the pack yesterday, I'm sure you'd have a good time. But it's your choice."

"Thank you. I really want to get this concoction and counter spell figured out. If we can make headway, that would be the best New Year's gift I can think of. I really hate that black witches have invaded our territory." Her jaw clenched and she balled her fists, thinking about the evil that had sunk its claws into her city. It made her mad every time she thought about it.

Dylan smiled. "Now, that I can understand and respect."

They found a high-end buffet spot with chef-made waffles, personal omelets, and a selection of bone-in meats. It was all delicious, and Caroline ate way more than she should've. But she wanted to try everything. Even the coffee was delicious.

After the meal, they swung by the pack house and picked up Miguel. His face lit up with a warm smile as he sat in the back with Caroline. She knew in her heart and soul he'd welcome her gladly in his pack den. "You know, we'd happily have you join us. You didn't come to my great state to only work."

She smiled. "I know. I just want to check on some things. I'm also worried about the people back home. If I can help figure this out, I feel I owe it to everyone to try."

He nodded. "I get that. Well, I've tried twice, and I'll respect your wishes. I packed a box of goodies for you, food, desserts, and drinks. I know drinking and science don't mix, but relax a little, it's a holiday." He bumped shoulders with her. "Since I hear you've eaten, make sure you get the goodies into the fridge when you get to the lab."

She took the bag from him and was surprised at its heft. He'd handled it so easily, but he was a werewolf, versus her simple witch strength. It made her feel a bit guilty for not attending his shing-dig, but she really wanted to spend as much time as she could in the lab. The care package ultimately made her feel like she belonged.

He gazed out the window. "I may call in an hour and try to convince you to come back. The snow is starting, and I don't want you stuck here too late." A few fat flakes drifted down past her window.

A shiver worked its way down her back. "How much snow is predicted?"

He got out his phone and checked. "There's a blizzard warning for two in the morning. You have a few hours. But, don't stay too late. Like I said, give us a call for pick up ... maybe an hour or two from now?"

"Okay. I will." She smiled. "Thank you ... for everything."

When they arrived at the compound, he walked her to the lab. "Okay, you're locked in. If you leave this area, you won't get back through, so ... you know the drill. And call. I mean it."

Once he was gone, she got to work. She didn't want to test their counter spells without Mazzy, they'd wait until Monday, but she checked them over. There were two that appeared promising. She spent some time taking notes on each of the twelve samples.

Done with her observations, she poured herself a glass of wine to celebrate an accomplishment. *No deed too small, and all that.*

While she was sitting on the couch halfway through her glass, the door slammed open. "What are you doing in my lab?"

Mazzy stormed in, looking like a goddess of hellfire. Her eyes practically glowed, making Caroline almost forget what she was doing. She took an extra moment to appreciate Mazzy's beauty. *Too bad she lives half a country away and has a stick up her ass about witches. She could be a good diversion otherwise.* Caroline sighed. "Right now? I'm drinking wine. Would you like a glass?"

"Would I? What? No! Why did you come here if all you're doing is getting drunk?"

Caroline smiled and wiggled her eyebrows, then took another sip. "I never said I was drunk. A few sips isn't enough for that. Would it be enough for you?"

The other woman gave her a 'what the fuck' look. "What are you doing here?" Mazzy spoke slowly as if Caroline were an idiot.

"I wrote my observations on the samples and debated how much wine I'd need to drink to test out a few of the more promising ones. You know, to be brave enough to face your beautiful wrath."

"You *what?*" This time she yelled.

"Kidding." Caroline lifted the hand that wasn't holding the wine. "I wouldn't test without you. But you're here now." A smile spread across her face, and she leaned forward. "Wanna run some tests?" She fluttered her eyelashes, trying to be enticing, then slumped, remembering who she spoke to. "Probably not. You're probably off to that party. What are you doing here, anyway?"

Mazzy's jaw dropped. "You're all over the place. I'm not sure you *can* hold your wine."

Caroline lifted the glass a bit higher. "Look at me, I'm holding it just fine." She snorted at her own lame joke.

"Right. No, I'm not going to the celebration. Like you, I'd rather figure out this counter-concoction. At least, I assume that's the real reason you're here. And as long as we're both here, why not?"

"Wine first. We need to celebrate my excellent notes." *Maybe wine will get her to loosen up, have a bit of fun.*

Mazzy rolled her eyes but agreed to a single glass of wine.

Chapter 23 - A Dime a Dozen
Mazzy

Mazzy didn't want to admit that she enjoyed sitting on the couch sharing a glass of wine with Caroline. Reminiscent of the night before, they fell into a comfortable discussion, talking about where they'd gone to college and how they each chose their educational focus.

Despite Caroline's love of biology and her own work in chemistry, they both had a love of all the sciences. Where Mazzy volunteered to tutor at least once a month, Caroline headed her department's help center, training tutors, and spending one to two nights a week helping students in both science and math.

Maybe I've been too harsh, assuming all witches are bad. Caroline's attractive ... and she called me beautiful, though, that was probably the wine. The woman can not hold her wine despite what she thinks.

Mazzy shook herself. *What am I thinking? I will not become enamored with a witch, especially one who lives in California!*

"Okay, about those samples ... ready to test them?" Mazzy placed her glass on the side table and stood. She needed to get her head back into the work.

"Sounds good. I have some theories about order, but it's your lab, and you are the chemist. What are your thoughts?"

Mazzy checked over the set-up. Everything looked good. The solutions had set the way they'd predicted. A quick scan of Caroline's notes revealed similar conclusions. "We could either test sets of four or do it by level of blood. Which would you prefer?"

Caroline stood on the other side of the lab table. "I think we should test them in sets of three. I know that means we'll have a higher failure rate, but if we get a hit, then we'll end up with a process of least resistance."

"If that's the case, then shouldn't we start with the four that don't involve any magic?"

Caroline's head bobbed back and forth as she thought about it. *I wonder if she knows how much the wine is affecting her.* "True. We could do that. The amount of energy for the two magic systems is pretty similar. Dealer's choice. Your lab, you decide."

"Okay, let's go with the four that don't use magic. If, by some miracle, one of them works, then we can produce the counter concoction without a slew of witches. With how tired you got, I can't imagine what it would do to you, or a couple of witches, to make a bigger batch." Mazzy's mine reeled at the idea.

"We'd need an entire coven. Spreading the power drain over a group would keep anyone from passing out. If we figure this out, then we can create a solution in Santa Cruz with my coven. That way the antidote is exactly where we need it."

The confidence in Caroline's voice that everything was possible impressed Mazzy. *Damn, this witch makes me feel like this could actually work. Why does she have to be beautiful and smart?* Mazzy shook her head. *Maybe the wine is affecting me, too.*

"Okay, let's do this."

Over the next hour, they worked through the four samples that were created without magic. They had to test the sample, mix it with some of the tainted tea, and then test the tea. Each step of the process took time.

Mazzy looked at the pitcher of tea, now about a quarter gone. "Any chance your alpha can get more of this? I mean, we're only using a bit each time, but this is a finite amount."

Caroline snorted. "My alpha? You know I'm not a wolf." She shook her head. "I can send her a text. Working at the same University doesn't guarantee we're friends, but as it goes, we are. We have lunch together, regularly. That said, I doubt she can get more of this." Caroline tapped the tea. "It was only dumb luck that we got that sample."

"Well, these four did nothing. The tea is eating our test subjects for lunch."

"We predicted that. Let's move on to the next set."

They started with each of the magic samples that didn't have any of the werewolf blood. Working in pairs, versus sets of four, took about forty to forty-five minutes. Writing up the notes took another five to ten.

After three hours, they only had two left. They decided to take a break and have some food. They dug into the goodies Miguel had sent with Caroline. Cheese and crackers, pastries, and sandwiches.

Caroline picked up a package of wrapped white cheese. She started to stack it with some crackers. "What kind of cheese is this?"

Mazzy looked up. "Gods above, he sent the Dubliner, that's my favorite. Is the Jarlsberg in there, too?"

Caroline took a dainty bite. Her eyes widened as her face lit up, electrifying her beauty. "This is amazing. I don't often buy cheese. I love it, but I get filled up so quickly."

With a snort, Mazzy made a double-decker cheese and cracker sandwich. She added some summer sausage. "You just need to wolf out, my friend." *Then you'd be just about perfect. Who else works instead of parties?*

Caroline snorted. "I can't believe you lowered yourself to call a witch your friend, but I'll take it."

Mazzy got up. "Okay, I'm going to go use the facilities, then we can do the last round."

"Sounds good. Maybe another celebratory round of wine; it's been hours."

"Sure, pour us each a glass. I'll be back in a minute."

Being a bit of a control freak, she circled through the lab and double checked the next samples. The last sample for the regular magic appeared fine, but the one for the Power of

Seven had an "off" smell. *Am I imagining things? Did the others have this same smell, and I just didn't notice? Maybe it's just the level of blood mixing with magic. I'll discuss it with Caroline before we mix this with the tea.*

On the way back from the lady's room, Mazzy got a text from Miguel. Are you safe? I assume you hadn't planned on coming to the festivities this year?

She gazed at her phone, then leaned against the wall to type. It wasn't in the plans. I'm at the lab with Caroline. We're almost done. I thought I'd take her to the hotel after that.

There was a pause as the text bubbles danced at the bottom of her screen. I don't know if I'm happy or upset you're there. She's not answering her texts. Have you checked outside? The overnight snow came early. You two aren't going anywhere.

Mazzy felt like she'd been punched in the gut. What? No! I'm not sleeping in the lab. Not with only one couch and a witch.

Yes, you are. There's a reason the couch pulls out into a bed. A reason there's a kitchen, fully stocked. She could feel her alpha's calming presence through their bond as she read his words. She wanted to reject them, but she knew that would be petulant of her.

So, what, I have to have a sleepover with a witch? She hoped all the frustration she felt reached her alpha.

The calm momentarily turned to amusement. Keep me informed of how things go. And, Mazzy, don't kill her.

She bit back a snarl as she stuffed her phone in a pocket. *Don't kill her. Right. Whatever. If he wanted her safe, he'd come pick her up.*

As she entered the room, she saw Caroline at the lab table mixing one of the concoctions with the tea.

She'd barely taken another step when the sample exploded.

Chapter 24 - Explosive ... Personality
Caroline

After cleaning up the kitchen and standing around for a few minutes, Caroline decided to get things started. It was late and she was tired. Miguel wanted her to leave hours earlier than this. She had Mazzy here, but really, they needed to get things moving.

Mixing the solutions with the tea wouldn't be the interesting part, it was analyzing what came next. If she got the blending part done, then when Mazzy returned, they could analyze, and she could get back to the hotel.

I can order some room service, read a book, and ring in the new year with a blast ... sleep.

She stretched, then measured out two portions of the tea. She put the tea back in the refrigerator and then moved back to the lab bench. First, she mixed the basic spell sample. On first glance, she was dubious. The reaction appeared to be the same as the last ten, but science was not about observation alone.

Moving that away, she took the last test tube, using a pipette, portioned out a measured amount of the solution. She heard Mazzy's footsteps as she let the drops fall into the petri dish with the tainted tea.

There was a bit of sizzling and bubbling, then a loud bang, as the reaction exploded in her face.

She threw her arms up, but it was too late. Pain seared across her neck as terrified chills invaded her body. She fell back, hitting the ground, as the world blurred.

Shit, shit, shit. She tried to push herself up, but her body trembled too much.

"Don't move!" Mazzy's commanding voice shot through her, and she froze. "Damn it all to hell, what were you doing, working without me?"

Caroline wanted to laugh. *If Mazzy had been here, it still would've exploded. I doubt she'd see it that way, though ... control-freak that she is.*

The gorgeous fiery brown eyes came into view, surrounded by a cascade of brown curls. "For fuck's sake, Caroline! You're bleeding."

As prickly as Mazzy was, her hands were gentle as she removed glass from Caroline's wounds. A wet towel wiped away blood.

"Gods above, you have a gash on your neck. We need a doctor to stitch you up. The petri dish flew into you. I can't even imagine ..."

Caroline's trembling got worse. "Okay, so we go to the hospital. It isn't that far, right?"

A low snarl stopped her babbling. "We can't go to the hospital. We're snowed in. It's just you and me."

"Oh." The world dropped out from under her as the reality of the situation sank in.

Mazzy grabbed her hand and placed it over the towel at her neck. "Hold this. I need to find a first aid kit."

The other woman stomped off, and Caroline collapsed back, holding the towel at her neck. She felt it go from dry to moist. That wasn't good. The room spun, thrumming with the pounding in her head. Her hand slipped. She tried to hold it to her neck, but it seemed like too much effort.

When she closed her eyes, the spinning got worse, but the pulsing got better. A trade-off.

"What are you doing? You need to keep pressure on your wound!" Mazzy sounded half frantic.

"Aren't I?" Caroline could've sworn that's what she was doing.

"No." She could feel the woman getting closer. Heard her sniff. "I need to get you bandaged up, but then I need to get a sample of your blood. I'm worried you were infected with what's in the tea."

Her mind floated on a cloud, then a piercing fear shot through her. Reality kicked in. "Not possible, there was only like a tablespoon in that petri dish. No way it could've gotten into me."

Mazzy huffed, then worked on patching up Caroline's neck. "It'll only hurt for a second."

She felt a sting on her arm. "Hey, do you even know how to use a needle?"

"Quiet. Let me work." The snap in Mazzy's voice had Caroline sinking back into herself and the quagmire of sensations around her.

Caroline cracked open an eye and stared at the beauty above her. "You're pretty. What are you working on?" She knew she should know, but everything was so fuzzy. *Why am I lying on the ground?*

Mazzy's cool hand touched her forehead. "Damn it, you're burning up. Okay, just give me a few minutes. Let me figure this out."

"No worries, I'm not going anywhere. I don't think I can." And it was true, though she wasn't sure why. *Was I drugged? Am I drunk?*

She lay in a haze of pain and confusion until Mazzy came back. "Caroline." A shake to her shoulder. "Caroline!" Louder this time. "Listen. You have the tainted black magic in your system. I don't know how fast it will affect you, but without a cure, you're going to have a heart attack."

Caroline squeezed her eyes shut, trying to follow all the words. She knew what each meant, but her brain couldn't string them all together.

Another shake. "Caroline, do you understand me?"

"Black magic. Heart attack." It felt like her insides were turning to stone. Her life ... it was over.

"What do you want?"

"Options." She couldn't think. She could barely follow what Mazzy said. Maybe with concrete ideas, her brain would kick in, and she'd know what to do.

The other woman sighed. "Well, you can die."

"Nope, don't like that one."

"Or, if my alpha agrees, I could make you a werewolf."

Like ice cold water splashing her, Caroline's mind restarted. A wolf. She'd lose her magic. She'd stop being a witch. She'd have to reinvent herself.

Don't be a fool. It's death or this. Magic is your identity, but life is more important than anything else. You'll still have science, you'll still have your brain, and Tamsin will welcome you into her pack ... probably.

A tear burned down the side of her face.

"I don't want to die."

Chapter 25 - A Whiteout, A Tempest, And A Really Bad Way to End the Year
Mazzy

What the hell happened? How could their solution and the black magic concoction cause an explosion? And was she really about to bite Caroline?

I have to talk to Miguel first.

She reached for her phone, but her hands were shaking. After a second fumble, she managed to pull the contraption from her pocket. It took more than one attempt to make the call.

"Mazzy, we just talked, what's up?"

"There was an explosion in the lab, nothing huge, but a piece of tainted glass sliced Caroline's neck."

Silence. And then: "I thought I told you not to kill the witch?" There was a pause, and he took in a deep breath. "Will she live?"

Mazzy gulped. That was the question, wasn't it? "I got the cut covered, but it needs stitches, and I'm no medic."

"You can do basic sewing, can't you?"

She wanted to shake the phone. "Miguel, listen. Her neck's bad enough, but some of the concoction entered her system. You know, the shit that's been killing people in Santa Cruz."

There was silence for a few seconds. "Fuck. Does that mean she's a dead witch walking?"

"Did you read any of the reports that Tamsin sent?" A low growl vibrated through the line. Anyone but a wolf wouldn't have heard. She knew her alpha registered the sound.

He sighed. "I skimmed them."

Strangle. She'd strangle him if he were there. He was an excellent alpha, fantastic at higher-level organization, but when it came to details ... "The black witches can't do magic on a large scale that works on werewolves. One of Tamsin's wolves saved a human by turning them."

She could feel his shock and trepidation through their bond. "Mazzy, have you spoken to her about this? She won't be a witch anymore."

"She knows. It's this or death. We don't have an antidote yet."

"How long from ingestion to death?"

"From the reports it can be minutes to days. There hasn't been a study as to the factors involved. Do we ... do *you* want to make that call?"

"Fuck! Gods above, no. Okay, if you have her acceptance. At least we know she knows what she's agreeing to. Does she want to be part of our pack, or stay in Santa Cruz?"

Mazzy's jaw dropped. "Really? That's what you're asking. Believe it or not, we didn't have that discussion. I don't know if she wants others knowing about this yet, so please, keep it to yourself for now."

"Of course. This is huge. We can figure things out later."

"Goodbye, Miguel. We'll talk tomorrow."

He snorted. "Talk with you next year!" He hung up before she could respond.

She knelt by Caroline. The witch was burning up. Not good. "Okay, Caroline. I'm going to shift to my wolf and bite you. It's going to hurt. Probably a lot. I've never done this, but I can't imagine it's pleasant."

"Fine, but you better promise a pleasant nibbling later."

Mazzy blushed. "If you survive, we can discuss."

"If? In that case, I demand a good luck kiss now."

Looking down at the other woman, Mazzy wondered if she even knew what she was saying. "A what now?"

"Oh, you heard me. You're beautiful, and I haven't been kissed since ... well, I don't remember. If this is it, I'd like a gorgeous woman to kiss me before the end. Not to mention, it's New Year's Eve. Don't we both deserve a kiss? I'm sure it's midnight somewhere. Woo!" She twirled her finger in the air with her last pitiful sounding word.

With a sigh and an eye roll, Mazzy helped Caroline up to a sitting position. She tottered, but they managed. Kissing the black haired beauty wasn't going to be a hardship. She cupped Caroline's face and leaned in.

Their innocent kiss deepened, and chills of desire shot through Mazzy's body, heating her. For a few moments, she lost herself, enjoying the taste of Caroline and the feel of her in her arms.

Once their kiss ended, Mazzy searched Caroline's blue eyes. She realized she wanted this witch to survive. "Do *not* die on me."

"Is that an order?"

"Yes. Now, I'm going to lay you back down and shift. Please survive."

"Yes, ma'am."

Mazzy quickly stripped off her clothes and started the change. It didn't take long to call on her brown wolf. She welcomed the pain as muscles, bones, and body morphed from one shape to another. The distraction let her growing connection to another person fade, even if only for a moment.

Once she stood on four paws, she moved to Caroline. She nosed the other woman's waist. *We didn't prepare well enough.*

Caroline laughed. "Ah, you want my help in your mauling of me. Where do you need access, beautiful?"

Mazzy tapped her twice. Once on the belly and a second time on her leg.

The other woman sighed and pushed down her pants then pulled up her shirt. Mazzy gazed at the half-naked woman. Only a small piece of black fabric covered her most private bits.

With a huff, she moved in and bit Caroline's side, making sure to mix her saliva with the witch's blood. *Soon to not be a witch. I'm fundamentally changing Caroline forever.*

A sadness filled Mazzy as she moved to Caroline's thigh and bit down again.

Caroline initially yelped in pain, but by the second and third bites, she just whimpered softly.

As quickly as she could, Mazzy shifted back. Hope and guilt warred in her. She wanted the transition to work, but didn't want Caroline to lose who she was, that which had defined her her whole life.

Her stomach told her its opinion about what should come next, but she ignored that. She dashed to the kitchen, rinsed her mouth, and then grabbed some towels, wet them down, and returned to Caroline. She cleaned up the mess. She didn't think Caroline waking up to see all that blood on her body would help.

As she wiped, she saw the wounds were already healing ... it had worked. The witch was becoming   a   wolf.

Chapter 26 - A Nice Surprise
Caroline

Everything hurt. Her head pounded. Her side felt like someone had been snacking on her, and her leg—gods! Was death such a bad option? *Is it too late?*

"Yes, it's too late. You're going to survive, and the pain should decrease. You're starting to heal."

"Am I speaking out loud or are you reading my mind?"

"I'm reading your mind." Mazzy's voice sounded flat and unamused. "Now relax and let your body heal."

Caroline, on the other hand, thought it was hilarious. She laughed. "Ouch. Owie! Don't make me laugh."

With a grunt, the other woman sat beside her. "I'm not trying to amuse you, I'm trying to get you mobile. I've just never done this, and I want you to be better." Stress laced Mazzy's voice.

Caroline shut her eyes and took stock of everything. She thought about who she was, her life as a witch, and how everything had changed in an instant. A wave of sadness engulfed her. She had to reinvent herself, but that was a problem for another day. Now that the pounding in her head had subsided, she grew more aware that the pain in her side also had receded.

"I think I am getting better. The pain seems to be going away, but the room wants to dance with me."

She heard rustling. "Let me get you some water and maybe some food."

Caroline's stomach rumbled. "Gods! Food sounds amazing. Is there any steak?"

A chuckle came to her from a distance. Caroline finally opened her eyes, and the room stayed put. She slowly moved her hands beneath her and pushed up. The room didn't flip or sway. *I guess it wants a different dance partner.*

Crossing her legs, she leaned forward, and pain exploded from her side. She whimpered.

Suddenly, Mazzy was beside her. "For fuck's sake! What are you doing? Why are you sitting up? You're going to make things worse for yourself."

"Water?"

Mazzy wrapped an arm around her and helped her to drink. After the first glass, she felt marginally better. Mazzy left and came back with the remains of the food from the New Year's fare Miguel had sent. Caroline started with a chocolate chip cookie and some juice. Well ... wine. She figured it was as close as she could get to what they served at a blood donation place.

Then Mazzy insisted on more water and protein.

Caroline ate more than she thought possible, but in the end, she finally felt stable enough to stand and move to a wingback chair next to the couch. She hesitated. "My undies are bloody, and I'm not wearing pants. I'll ruin the chair."

Mazzy shook her head. "Hold on." She left and came back with a towel and placed it on the chair. "Better?"

"Yeah. I don't know how you kept my shirt clean."

"It's called cleaning things up. It's not hard." Caroline could hear the edge of snark in Mazzy's voice and just smiled at her.

Sitting, she shifted a bit. "I can't believe I'm not hurting as bad as before. And my leg feels good as new."

One side of Mazzy's mouth twitched up. "Welcome to werewolf healing. Now, is there anything else you want before I set up the bed so we can sleep?"

"Some tea, if that's possible. Chamomile or peppermint, or a combination of the two."

Mazzy's face scrunched up. "I don't know that we've ever stocked tea, but maybe. I'll see what we have."

Cabinets opened and closed. "I found some black cherry tea. I'm guessing that's Kaitlyn's. Is that okay?"

"Sure, as long as it's tea. Something warm without caffeine."

Caroline closed her eyes, trying to relax. Mazzy's voice came at her again, from the kitchen. "Do you want anything in your tea? Sugar, milk, cream? Is cream a thing people put in tea?"

Caroline snorted. "Just the tea. Nothing added."

While Mazzy made the tea, Caroline thought about how quickly her body healed. *It's amazing, but the trade-off is the loss of my magic. I can no longer adjust the temperature of the tea when Mazzy brings it to me too hot or too cold.* She thought about the beautiful scientist. *And I'm sleeping here with her tonight.* A shiver ran through her body, and she didn't want to analyze if it was anticipation or dread.

Mazzy placed the mug on the small table next to the chair. Steam billowed from the top. From the looks of it, the temperature prohibited safe tea drinking anytime soon.

As was her habit, Caroline dug deep into her water magic and waved her hand to cool the liquid so she could drink it right away.

A pain of remorse stabbed through her as she let her hand drop. Eyes closed, she slumped in the chair and sighed. *Well, it isn't like anyone expects me to adjust to being a wolf and not a witch overnight.*

"You okay?" The concern in Mazzy's voice brought Caroline out of her stupor.

"Yeah. I just ... it's nothing."

"No, it's something. You'll learn this soon enough, but smelling strong emotions is a thing. Tonight's been rough on you, I get it, but you have enough going on. If you can release some of what's in that head of yours, do."

"I just tried to use some magic to cool the mug of tea. It's hot. Too hot to drink. I have ... *had* ... water as a proficiency. Cooling a mug to the proper temperature is ... *was* ... child's play. It'll take time, and probably a lot of frustration on my part to adjust to not using magic, that's all." She fought a lump in the back of her throat, forcing herself to breathe around it. Tears pricked her eyes.

Mazzy walked over. "Sorry, I don't know how to make tea. I didn't realize there was a 'too hot.'"

"Not your fault."

"I can put it in the fridge for a couple of minutes. That may help." Caroline shrugged as Mazzy picked it up and froze. "Caroline, it isn't hot." She handed the mug to her.

Hands shaking, Caroline took a sip. It wasn't the flavor she wanted, but it may have been the best tasting tea she'd ever drank. She put the cup down and then waved her hand over the remaining liquid. It lifted up like a liquid snake, curled around her hand without touching it, and then slithered back into the mug.

With wide eyes, Caroline gaped up at Mazzy. "Am I going to die?"

Chapter 27 - A New Player in Town
Mazzy

Mazzy sat on one of the lab stools. Caroline paced, for all the world healthy and hale. "I don't get it. I healed, so that means I'm a werewolf. But I did water magic, so I'm a witch. I can't be both."

"Are you sure?"

"Yes. There's only one person who is both, and she was born of a witch and a werewolf. That's such a rare coupling that the combination is unheard of. When witches are turned, they lose their magic."

"But are you sure?" Mazzy asked again.

Caroline blew out a breath, shrinking into herself a bit. "You have a full research facility here; can't *you* figure it out?"

Mazzy sighed. "Probably, but finding the right reference material would take me more time than I want to spend at the moment. If we wait until tomorrow or Tuesday, Gus or Thomas can find the information spectacularly fast. It's what they do."

The other woman looked lost. "Okay, is there a way to test if I'm a wolf?"

"Besides the fact that you've healed the bite wounds?" The look of desperation pulled at Mazzy's soul. "I'm sorry. I know this is hard for you. The only other way to know is if you shift."

In the center of the lab, Caroline rubbed her face with her hands. Then her arms dropped to her sides and her eyes looked wild.

"What about smell? Can't you sniff me? Wouldn't that tell you if I'm a werewolf?"

"Yes and no. Once you've had your first shift, you'll take on the woodsy animal smell of wolf that other werewolves can scent. But you haven't had your first shift. You still smell like a witch. I thought it was your clothes, but now I don't know. I'd be curious to speak with your packmates about their pack member who's both a witch and a wolf. What does she smell like, I wonder?"

Caroline walked to the kitchen and grabbed the bottle of wine. It was almost gone. She didn't bother with a glass, just started drinking what was left.

"What are you doing?"

"I want to forget tonight. I'm tired and feel weird, and everything about my life is probably going to change. I don't know what's going to happen when I return to California. I just want to pass out."

Mazzy leapt up, took the bottle, and wrapped the other woman in her arms. Caroline sank into the hug like a kid who'd fallen on the playground and was desperate for the healing touch of a parent.

I want to be that person Caroline can rely on, who she turns to when she needs comfort. Shaking her head, Mazzy wondered where that thought came from. They barely knew each other. "Why don't we get into bed and try to get some sleep?" Mazzy mumbled into the other woman's hair. "I know your mind is going a million miles an hour, but you do need sleep. Your body has gone through a lot tonight."

"Can we test my blood for the black magic concoction? I just ... I ... I don't know if I can sleep if we don't."

Mazzy nodded into her hair. The scent of tea tree oil she must have in her hair product smelled good and Mazzy was momentarily distracted. "Of course. Let's do that and then try to sleep."

She led Caroline to a stool and sat her down. As she prepared her arm for a blood draw, Caroline's brows knit together. "Have you done this before? You seem to know what you're doing."

One of Mazzy's brows rose. "I do. I used to be a phlebotomist. It paid my way through college."

Caroline seemed to relax. She gazed around the lab. "You cleaned while I was down for the count. You can't tell there was a monumental mishap."

Mazzy wasn't sure if she wanted to growl or roll her eyes. "It's what I do best. Research and clean up messes. Now hold still, you're going to feel a pinch."

They'd gotten good testing for the heart attack concoction, and it didn't take long to determine that Caroline's blood was clean. She slumped, then turned to the bed and tensed. "There's only one bed."

Mazzy wrapped an arm around Caroline's shoulder. "You're a wolf now. Sleeping in a dog-pile is totally a thing. No worries."

In the back of her mind, Mazzy was very worried. Though they'd only kissed, her body sang at the idea of lying beside Caroline. As long as they each stayed on their own side of the bed, everything would be a-okay.

Chapter 28 - Happy New Year!
Caroline

Caroline couldn't remember a morning she'd woken up feeling better. She rolled to her back and stretched. Then she turned to her side and gazed into a pair of intensely brown eyes. Her heart sped up. She was a little breathless as she said, "Good morning."

Mazzy grunted, "What makes it so good?"

Feeling alive in a way she never had, Caroline smiled mischievously and leaned down slowly. If Mazzy didn't want a kiss, she'd give the other woman ample time to back away.

She didn't.

Their mouths met, hesitantly at first. A flash of heat surged through Caroline as she slid her hand up the side of the other woman's face to dig her fingers into her unruly curls. She traced her tongue along Mazzy's mouth, asking for entrance, and when she got it, she sank into the kiss, a new world of taste and sensation opened up to her.

Caroline pushed her body closer. Her tongue explored the inside of Mazzy's mouth as fire ignited her soul. She moaned and lost herself in the feel of the other woman's body below her.

She pulled away with a whimper, not wanting the moment to end, but wanting so much more. "Is this okay?"

"Yes." Mazzy's voice was husky with sleep and desire.

Caroline had slept in her T-shirt and her undies. She was asleep before Mazzy had slipped under the covers, but it appeared she was similarly clad.

It was still too much.

"Can I remove some of your clothing? It's getting in my way."

"Yes, gods, yes," the other woman breathed out in a low, throaty voice.

They each stripped down and met for a continuation of their kiss, legs intertwining so more of their bodies touched, connected, and rubbed together.

Caroline groaned. She let her hand smooth down Mazzy's neck to her shoulder, then lower, cupping her perfect breast. Her hand tingled with the contact. A shiver of excitement spread through her.

She rubbed her thumb over the taut nipple, stimulating it to tighter attention.

Trailing kisses down Mazzy's neck, Caroline made her way down until she could slip the other succulent breast into her mouth, circling the tip with her tongue, sucking the end between her teeth.

Beneath her, Mazzy lifted up, moaning. She rubbed her sex against Caroline's leg, heat building between them.

Caroline scraped her teeth over Mazzy's nipple, then kissed down her defined abs. Just the sight of Mazzy's perfect physique sent waves of heat through Caroline's body. So freaking sexy. She wanted to lick every inch of Mazzy.

Moving lower, she reached her prize. Sliding a finger into Mazzy, she found her slick and hot. A small groan encouraged her as Mazzy's hips moved with her actions. She removed her finger and, gazing into Mazzy's dark brown eyes, she licked off her fingers. "You taste divine. I want to eat you up."

Mazzy dropped her head back, lifted her hips, and growled.

Accepting the invitation, Caroline dipped her head and sucked on Mazzy's most private spot. Plunging one and then a second finger in, she set a slow but steady rhythm. Her tongue circled Mazzy's clit, then flicked it. She lost herself in the sounds the woman below her made. Her thrusts got faster, letting her tongue explore further, move quicker, tasting every inch of the wolf. With her newly enhanced senses, she could dine here for hours.

As she devoured Mazzy, the other woman cried out, bucking up and panting. She growled, "Gods above, no more! Come, kiss me."

Wanting to purr, Caroline crawled back up, rubbing herself against Mazzy like a cat claiming what they wanted. She kissed Mazzy, again lost in the sensations.

Mazzy flipped them so they lay face to face, her hand rubbing down Caroline's body. Caroline's body thrummed with desire as she panted. Every move turned her on. When Mazzy's finger began playing with her clit, it didn't take long for her world to explode. She couldn't remember an orgasm ever taking over her body quite so thoroughly before.

Once she returned to her senses and could think, she laid curled up with Mazzy, her arm slung across the other woman's waist. She could stay there forever, pull-out couch bed or not.

Chapter 29 - Where There's a Will There's a Way
Mazzy

Caroline fell back asleep, her head nestled on Mazzy's chest. The morning wake-up call was a shock and mind-blowing. Mazzy tightened her arms around

Caroline. Something in her clicked, like puzzle pieces fitting together.

How can a witch mesh so well with me? A wolf and a witch, but still ... a witch?

She decided not to question it and just enjoy the other woman.

Next to her Caroline hummed and stretched. "Is it morning or afternoon?"

"It's still morning."

"Why am I so hungry?"

Mazzy chuckled. "Let's go raid the kitchen, see what we can find. Then we'll check the level of the snow and see if we can get out of here."

Caroline sighed. "As hungry as I am, a shower sounds amazing, too."

"Would you want to come back to my place? I know that sounds fast, but I'm guessing Easton and Dylon wouldn't mind a few days alone."

There was a moment where Caroline gaped at her, and Mazzy wanted to yank her words back and swallow them down. *What was I thinking? We had fun this morning, but what do I know about his woman? Maybe she has sex with any woman she finds herself in bed with.*

"Yes. I mean, I don't want to intrude. But, that would be ... yes, I would love that."

Warmth blossomed in Mazzy's chest. Her wolf howled her agreement, but she suppressed that, not wanting to think about that side of herself. One step at a time. She enjoyed her morning. She was enjoying Caroline. But in a day or two she'd return to California. Right now, she needed to let herself live a little, just like her pack always told her to do.

Mazzy got up and found her clothes. "Before we leave, we should figure out if you have all of your magic or just a portion. Also, how you have it."

She heard the rustling sounds of Caroline getting dressed. "I wonder if I'm really a werewolf or only have some of the healing properties."

"That's also a good question. We should brainstorm each step of the process and try to determine what may have happened to you."

Caroline's stomach growled. "Agreed, but over food."

They found cereal in the cupboard and milk in the fridge. They poured bowls and sat at the small kitchen table with a pad of paper. "Okay," Mazzy said. "Assuming you're like that wolf in Santa Cruz, and can shift to a wolf and still maintain your magic, let's figure out what happened."

Caroline scraped the bottom of her bowl. "I don't even know if I tasted that."

Mazzy chuckled at her. "Just pour another bowl. You'll get used to the need for extra food. With the increase in healing, as well as moving more, you'll burn more calories. You grow accustomed to eating more to maintain regular levels of energy."

"Okay, right. I guess I've never seen an unfit werewolf. More cereal it is."

Taking the pad, Mazzy wrote: *Witch. Black witch concoction mixed with Power of Seven magic. Intravenous injection. Mixed with werewolf bite.* "Did I miss anything?"

Caroline looked at the list. "That looks complete. I wonder which piece was the most important part."

Mazzy traced her finger over each item. "My guess is that the Power of Seven is the key that let you maintain your powers. Even if all you have is your water magic, that's more than any other bitten witch has kept. At least as far as I've heard, and I have this research center."

"It's more than I've heard of either." Caroline took another bite of her cereal. "I got a stack of books from Katt's place. I wonder if there's anything in them I can reference."

Mazzy stood to wash her bowl and then put it away. "I'd love to see those books. I know they'd be top secret, or beyond my knowledge, but the idea of them is intriguing."

"Do you mind if I make some coffee?" Caroline stood, leaving her bowl on the table.

"Not at all; coffee sounds great. Are you done eating?" Mazzy couldn't take her eyes off the empty bowl left behind.

Swiveling around, Caroline looked at Mazzy and then at what she focused on. "Oh, yeah, I thought about another bowl, but I think I'm good for a bit. I'll get it in a few minutes. Don't worry. I just really want some coffee."

Mazzy shook herself. *Not everyone is as quick to clean as I am. Just breathe, Mazzy, it'll be fine.* She forced herself to sit and watch the other woman move around the kitchen. It took a few minutes, but she got the coffee started and then picked up her bowl.

After turning and seeing Mazzy's face, Caroline quickly whipped back around to the sink and cleaned her bowl. She wasn't sure what Caroline saw, but it was enough.

Maybe I shouldn't be as persnickety ... naw!

Coffee mugs in hand, they discussed setting up a new experiment. Caroline walked to the bench. "We never got the last set observed. Why don't we set up a series with your blood and the Power of Seven?"

"We can do that, but I also want to check out your powers. I've never worked with witches. Is there a way to determine what power you have?"

Caroline flopped onto a stool. "There is. It's easier with another witch, though. I think we should hold off."

"I have to ask. If you find out you are a full werewolf, what will you do?"

The other woman slumped. "I don't know. I mean, Tamsin will take me in as one of her own, I'm sure."

Mazzy nodded. "As I see it, you have a few options. That pack, our pack, or you could try being a lone wolf ... but that's a really hard path to take. I wouldn't suggest it."

Caroline looked up, eyes wide. "Your pack? Like move here? Relocate to Colorado Springs?"

The heat started in Mazzy's gut, but she refused to back down. "It's an option. I mean, you have your life, your coven, your job, but I just wanted you to have all possibilities laid out in front of you."

"I mean, what would I even do for work?"

Mazzy gazed around the lab. "I don't know. A brilliant wolf with a scientific mind ... wherever could she find a job around here?"

Caroline licked her lips. "I'll keep that on the list. I never thought about moving away from Santa Cruz."

"You also never thought about becoming a werewolf."

Caroline sighed. "True. This new year is really going to be ... new. I guess my resolution should be to not lose it!"

Mazzy laughed as they started setting up their new test solutions.

Chapter 30 - What's That Smell?
Caroline

Caroline's head started to pound, and her belly gurgled. "I can't believe I'm saying this, but I'm hungry again."

Mazzy looked up from finishing the setup. "Well, it's a good thing we're done here. Let's go check on the outside world, see if it's traversable."

"That sounds great. I would give a lot for food and a shower."

One of Mazzy's eyebrows rose. "What exactly would you give in trade? I feel I'm at a distinct advantage here."

Moving over to the gorgeous woman, Caroline wrapped her arms around her waist, and bent for a kiss. "At this point, anything. You name it, it's yours."

A low sound—a purr? a growl?—came from Mazzy. She leaned in and bit Caroline's earlobe. "I like the sound of that. Come on, let's go pick up your stuff from the hotel, then I'm taking you home with me." There was a pause before Mazzy's head tilted to the side. "You aren't allergic to cats, are you?"

A laugh burst from Caroline. "You have a cat? You are full of surprises. No, I am not allergic. I like furry creatures ... apparently a lot."

They headed out of the lab area. Once in the parking lot, Colorado Springs looked like someone had tucked it in under a clean white comforter. The one eyesore breaking up all the clean snow were the plowed roads. "It looks like we're free. But we'll have to scrape off my car. Do you, with your California blood, know how to do that?"

Caroline barked out a laugh. "I think I can figure it out and help."

It took about a quarter of an hour to find enough car to call it safe to drive and then they were off. The hotel wasn't far from the pack house, and the research center wasn't far from either location.

They found both Easton and Dylan watching TV in the living room. Dylan smiled at Caroline and gave Mazzy a confused look. "Happy New Year!"

Easton got up to give Caroline a hug. Before he reached her, he stopped and smelled the air. "Caroline, you smell different. Did something happen last night?"

She blushed and then shot a glance over her shoulder at Mazzy. "Nothing you need to hear about. I'm going to go pack my bag and stay with Mazzy tonight. She'll give you her address.

You can pick me up tomorrow before we head out to get Katt and Jett."

Dylan perked up. "Does that mean you figured things out in the lab?" His gaze bounced back and forth between the two of them.

Caroline shut her eyes for a moment as she slumped. "No, it means I realize that we're scheduled to leave tomorrow, and we've done what we can today. You need to get home before the full moon." *And so do I.* "You can pick me up at Mazzy's on the way to getting Jett and Katt in Denver."

Dylan's face softened, and he gave a small smile to Mazzy before speaking to Caroline. "You know, we don't have to be back on Wednesday. Thursday would be fine, and I'm sure Katt would love another day with her family. If you're making headway at the lab, take another day."

Easton smiled wickedly. "Not to mention, you taking another day gives Dylan and I a mini-vacation together. He won't mention it, but I will. We can go out to the park, run, then come back and—"

Caroline threw up her hands. "You know, I get it. You live in a house with a ton of people. A vacation in a hotel is a nice change. Let me grab my things, and you two can have a couple days to just be alone together."

Behind her, Mazzy chuckled.

When they got to Mazzy's apartment complex, Caroline froze, then sneezed. She rubbed her nose. "Oh, gods, what's that smell?"

With a shrug, Mazzy propelled Caroline towards the stairs. "It smells like my neighbor is cooking curry."

"But I love curry."

"Probably, but you're smelling a lot more now."

"But it wasn't like this in the lab, or at the hotel. What's happening to me? Gods above, Mazzy, I'm tearing up."

Mazzy slid her arm around Caroline's back and gave her a squeeze. "You were in two sterilized environments. This is different. We're in the real world now. Come on."

Caroline thought her eyes would roll to the back of her head as they went up a flight of stairs. She could barely make out the door numbers. The shiny twenty-seven C was a watery blur as Mazzy pushed her through and shut the door.

A calm settled over her as soon as the assault on her nose was shut away.

Mazzy smiled. "I've worked to create a calm, scent-free environment here. It took a bit of work, but it was that or move to a small, detached home. And I like my apartment."

"I don't blame—"

A flash of orange slammed into Caroline's ankle followed by what she assumed was a vehicle's motor. She leaned down and picked up the monster of a cat, whose purring only got louder. *Goodness this creature is huge ... and demanding. It's a roommate all by itself!*

Mazzy's grin widened. "Meet Dennis. He's every bit the menace you'd expect with his given name. He rules the roost."

"I'm sure you do, you orange beastie," she mumbled. A bit louder, she said, "He must be hungry. I can't believe you weren't more worried about him." Caroline took a step, but didn't know which direction the cat's food was in.

"Nah, I have an auto-feeder. With my schedule and full moon night runs, it's easier to automate his feeding than worry about His Majesty missing a meal."

Relief flooded Caroline. She hadn't realized how worried she'd been for the beast. "Good, so since he's gotten food, that leaves us. Food, shower, and ..." She paused. "Do you have any games we can play? Or would you like to watch a movie?"

"I have some card games. Why don't you go take a shower while I get food going?"

Gently placing the monster of a cat down, Caroline drifted towards the bathroom in a bemused state. *How did I end up here? Everything feels so perfect ... so right.*

Chapter 31 - Last Hurrah
Mazzy

The next morning, they woke up early to get to the lab. It was the last day to work on things before Caroline headed back to California. Mazzy went into the bathroom to brush her teeth and start the shower.

A loud crash came from the bedroom. "Everything okay in there?"

"Yeah! I, uh ... dropped my shirt."

Mazzy's eyebrow shot up, not certain she understood the physics of the situation. "Your shirt? Fell?"

"Well, yeah. I may have been in it at the time."

Mazzy had to bite her bottom lip to stop from laughing. Toothpaste dripped down her chin. She quickly spit it out and rinsed. "Ah, are you okay?"

Caroline walked in, a towel wrapped around her, a clean outfit slung over her arm. "Yeah, I'm good. I'm ready for a shower, food, and work. I still feel ... odd, but I'm getting better."

"I think you feel fantastic," Mazzy purred.

Smiling, Caroline dropped her towel with much less sound than the shirt.

They both stepped into the shower. Caroline took the bar of soap, pressed her wet body against Mazzy, and leaned in for a kiss. She rubbed the soap up and down Mazzy's back while probing her mouth with her tongue.

I never knew getting clean could be so exciting. Heat built in her belly as their bodies slid against each other.

After a few moments, she pulled back and dragged the soap slowly over Mazzy's shoulder and across her collar bone. The warm water sluiced the suds away. Caroline leaned down to kiss the clean skin.

She repeated the process over each bit of skin, giving extra attention to Mazzy's breasts. The heat spread, burning throughout Mazzy's body at the slow seduction. A growl slipped out when Caroline's teeth teased her nipples.

This woman will be the death of me!

The other woman knelt, continuing to clean lower. She paid special attention to all areas between Mazzy's legs. Once the water had time to clear the suds away, Caroline's magic gave her a respite from the water hitting her face. It looked like an invisible umbrella protected her. She leaned in to nibble and suck while her hands rubbed up and down each leg with the soap.

Caroline's tongue dove deep, probing Mazzy. One sudsy hand slid back to clean

Mazzy's ass, and her other hand slid up to play with a breast.

Mazzy leaned against the shower wall, her world all the places Caroline touched her. Her thoughts fizzled out as she descended into a sea of sensations. The warm water beat down on her in a counterpoint.

Caroline licked up, grazing her teeth over Mazzy's clit, and she broke, stars taking over her vision. Barely able to stop herself from toppling over, she breathed out Caroline's name.

All the samples failed, making Mazzy want to scream. *Damnit! Why can't we undo or cure what the damn black witches created! We have to be smarter than those maniacal assholes!*

Kaitlyn looked over Mazzy and Caroline's notes and sighed. "So, you say one of the samples exploded?"

Mazzy nodded. "Yeah, that's what ..." She paused and looked at Caroline, sadness hitting her at the number of times she'd have to explain her new situation.

Caroline sighed. Mazzy knew she'd asked Miguel to keep her status a secret so even though it was Kaitlyn's lab, too, she didn't know. The new wolf wasn't ready to explain to anyone that Mazzy had bitten her to save her life, not until after the full moon and she knew the full consequences of the action.

Emotions played over the other woman's face. Finally she huffed out a breath and shook her head. "Gah! Fine, okay, here is the situation..." She rubbed her face, then explained everything to Kaitlyn. "I don't want people knowing about any of this until after the full moon, but since this is your lab, you need to know all the details. I assume you can keep it quiet."

Kaitlyn's mouth hung open. "You almost died on New Year's Eve and only Miguel knows about it?"

"I know, it isn't fair of me to ask this of you, it's just..." Caroline looked like she floundered as brows furrowed and her hands waved around.

After putting up her own hands, Kaitlyn tried to reassure her. "No, it isn't that, it's just Miguel, he's horrible at keeping secrets. I mean, ones that would endanger the pack yeah, but things like this, he's the biggest gossip I know. And the man got drunk that night, or as drunk as a wolf *can* get. Wow. This is ... okay, let's move on. You may be a wolf. Wouldn't the loss of your magic," Kaitlyn started ticking things off on her fingers, "the healing of your wounds and Mazzy's bites, and your increased appetite be some clues? Not to mention, any other changes? Like, smells. And are you clumsy with a new balance point, you know, center of gravity?"

Kaitlyn's eyes widened as she gazed at Caroline. She looked as if she wanted to see inside the other woman for answers.

Caroline gulped. "Yes to all of that, except I haven't lost my magic. Well, I haven't tested all of it. I can't do that alone—not easily. I know I haven't lost all of it."

Kaitlyn dropped onto a stool and gaped. "Okay, I'm out of my depth. With magic involved, I have no idea what's going on.

Would you be okay with me taking some of your blood to study? Not to play with right now, but maybe next week? I'd like to see if I can determine any similarities between, say, Mazzy's blood, your blood, and Alice's blood. Alice was bitten, too."

With a groan, Caroline nodded. "I mean, I guess. But then I'd like to focus on the black magic concoction. Today is my last day here and our last chance to use the Power of Seven spells with the mixtures. I did some studying last night, and I have an idea I think will work. And my hope is that I have enough power to do it."

If this doesn't work, I'm not sure what we can do.

Chapter 32 - Tail As Old As Time
Caroline

Caroline shut her book and put it on the seat next to her. Her head was stuffed with all the runes and theories she tried to learn.

She grunted and leaned against the window, watching the fields and trees fly by. The landscape wasn't very interesting during this part of the drive. They had just over six hours and they'd be home. *Gods above, if I turn furry, will I be allowed to keep my home? Do I have to move into that damn pack house? What are the rules? Maybe I should've paid more attention.*

With a big sigh, she rubbed her face and glanced back at Jett, then forward to the men in the front seat. There were experts available ... *just do it, Caroline. Get the information you need.*

"So, do all the werewolves from your pack live in the pack house?" She thought she sounded nonchalant.

Easton yawned before swiveling to face her. "No, not everyone. Jett lives in the dorms. Wynn has her own house, as does Cyrus. We don't know where Mil will end up living. Hell, our last alpha used to live in your very own coven house since he was married to a witch ... though he spent a lot of time at the pack house."

Gah! Her mind was scattered. How could she forget? She knew that. The death of first Clyde, their former alpha, and then Elinore, one of Caroline's former dearest friends, brought Tamsin back to Santa Cruz from Chicago in the first place.

Jett leaned forward. "But every wolf seems to have a room. I have a space all my own, so when the dorms closed, I had a place to go. I'll also have a place over the summer. I have to decide what I want to do next fall. My scholarship covers a dorm room, and it's nice living on campus, but living with teens is rough."

Caroline laughed. "I can imagine. I work with them. I wouldn't want to live with them."

Katt chuckled. "I have a similar setup at the coven house. Cinthia gave me a room that I can use when I don't want to stay in the dorms."

"What about during the full moon? Does everyone have to run with the alpha? Is that why our return was so important?"

Easton tilted his head. "It's nicer to run with the pack, especially a strong alpha, and Tamsin is an excellent alpha. We could've stayed in Colorado or stopped somewhere along the way, but the full moon is Saturday and, as you said, classes start Monday. Having a few days to decompress from the trip is nice for all you college people."

"Okay, but do you need to shift for the full moon?" This was one of Caroline's biggest fears. What if she was a wolf, missed the fact that there was a full moon, and shifted in front of normal humans? A pit opened in her stomach, bile filling the back of her throat.

Dylan gazed at her through the rear view mirror. "We do. One night, when the moon is at its brightest. She calls to us. The run is magical, a privilege. We can run other nights, but that night is a must." His eyes shifted between the road and her. "Are you okay? You've lost color, and your smell has changed."

Her throat closed as she tried to get air. Arms trembling, she fisted her hands, nails biting into her palms. She licked her lips. "I'm fine."

Easton barked out a laugh. "I would let that slide, if we didn't have hours to sit with you in a car with you as a mess. I'm seriously worried. Did you know that werewolves can hear a lie? We can smell your emotions? Not all wolves, but we're old, and you're emoting ... loudly."

Jett snorted. "You're not that old."

Easton shook his head as the car continued down the road.

Shutting her eyes, Caroline gave in to the inevitable. "I'm sorry, I just ... I don't want people to know. Not yet. Not until *I* know. I mean, I'll have to tell Tamsin, but ... I was hoping to wait until next week. Maybe never."

Jett touched her shoulder and a sense of peace flowed through her. It made no sense, but she could finally breathe. Shifting her eyes to first Jett and Katt, then Eason and Dylan, she nodded. "Okay, here's what happened on New Year's Eve."

Once she finished telling her story, the car was silent for a few moments.

"Fuck!" Dylan said softly, the word filled with frustration and resignation. He swerved around a slow driver. "You've been keeping this to yourself?" He caught Caroline's gaze in the rearview mirror, and she nodded at him. "First rule of pack: we're family. We're here for you. You aren't alone." There were murmurs of agreement from the others.

From the back, Katt said, "You were bitten, but you still have magic?" There was a bit of hope in her voice.

"Yes, but I don't know how much. I couldn't test it alone."

Katt started to reach her hand forward. "I could help you. We could figure it out together."

Dylan cleared his throat. "Before you do that, a few things. Will it interrupt my driving? I don't want a weird magic show distracting me, I have enough buzzing through my mind right now." His voice was stern, as the number of cars seemed to grow.

Easton shook his head at his husband. "Caroline, I'm sure you're freaking out. I would be. I'm glad you were asked, and you knew a bit about what it meant to be changed, but you're still way behind in the training that new wolves get. We could've spent the last few days giving you information if we'd known. I wish you'd opened up earlier. We do have time now."

Her eyebrow rose. "I don't know if twenty hours of intense werewolf lessons sounds like my idea of the best car time ever. But maybe the next few hours."

He bobbed his head. "Okay, fair enough. But you have to make sure Tamsin knows."

"That's top of my list. Then Cinthia. Depending on timing, maybe the other way around, but they'll both know right away. But beyond them, I don't want to share this with anyone until after I know if I turn furry."

The car went quiet for a few moments. Then Katt spoke up again. "Our testing shouldn't be visible to you, Dylan. It's mostly mental. Why don't you give us a few minutes, maybe fifteen?"

Caroline narrowed her eyes. "Or a half hour, just to be on the safe side. I have no idea what's going on in here." She tapped her head.

"Okay. A half hour," Katt agreed. "Then she's all yours."

Caroline shifted so she sat comfortably. Katt put her hands on either side of her head. Once she shut her eyes, she could feel the other witch settling in. Caroline had done the magic test a few times because of her mental proficiencies. She pushed out her skills, giving

Katt a bit of the power to manipulate. The other woman made a small happy sound as she utilized the helpful oomph to do her search.

Slowly, a rainbow of colors flashed behind Caroline's eyes, representing the different aspects of magic. *What am I doing? This is Katt's show. I can relax and let Katt do all this probing!* Caroline sighed in contentment as she let the younger woman continue to do her work.

The testing showed Caroline still had all her magic. A wave of relief washed through her when they determined that she could probe memories and do the basics of everyday magic. From her time with Mazzy, she knew she could manipulate water. She shook her head, dumbfounded. "It has to be the Power of Seven mixed in my blood at the time of the wolf bite."

Jett looked asleep when she said, "Or the combination of the black magic, Power of Seven, and the wolf bite. It seems like a pretty risky combination to try to randomly test."

Next to her, Katt sighed.

Before Easton began the wolf lessons, Jett sat up and stared at Caroline as if she could see into her.

Caroline gazed back. "What?"

"I'm just wondering if your blood is the key we've been looking for to cure this black magic infestation."

Chapter 33 - Not Just a River in Egypt
Mazzy

After sweeping the floor for the third time, Mazzy walked heavily to the kitchen trash to dump out the dust. Her footsteps echoed in the large room. She glared at her books. Too many thoughts swirled in her head like a whirlwind for her to be able to focus, she needed to move.

The obvious solution: cleaning. At the sink, she found a rag and a bottle of cleaning solvent and started in on the counters. *Gah! This place is a mess. When was the last time anyone cleaned?*

"Mazzy, stop," Kaitlyn snapped. "You're going in circles. That is the fifth time you cleaned that counter today. If you clean it any more, it'll disintegrate."

Pausing to look down, Mazzy shook her head. "What?"

Kaityln sighed, put down her work, and came into the kitchen. "You've been stomping around the lab, cleaning for hours. You're distracted and not doing anything useful. We're either going to talk this out, or you're leaving. A run in the woods out back could help a little. Maybe if Miguel went with you it'd be better. But you're spiraling out of control here."

What the hell is she talking about? Spiraling? I'm fine! "I'm not. This place is just a mess and needs a bit of TLC."

Kaitlyn grabbed her shoulders and gave a small shake. "No, it doesn't need a bit of tender love and care. You do. You don't even see what's happening in front of you."

"What's ... what do *you* think is happening?" An edge crept into her voice.

"It's not what I think, Mazzy, it's what I see. You and Caroline connected, on a wolf level."

Mazzy scoffed. "No, she was a fun diversion for the New Year, that's it. She's gone, and I'm moving on."

Kaitlyn's eyes softened. "Do you really believe that? Does your wolf?"

"Yes," Mazzy snarled. "I have to. What else can I do? She's gone. She left me here and went back to her life as a witch. A fucking witch, Kaitlyn. How can I even begin to think about allowing myself to fall for a witch?"

Strong arms wrapped around her in a soul healing-hug. Kaitlyn pulled back, her hands staying on Mazzy's arms, rubbing up and down. "It isn't about allowing, it's about our souls finding the one that complements us. Sometimes we fall in love and it's fantastic. Sometimes we find the piece of ourselves that was missing, and our soul, our person, and wolf souls feel complete."

Mazzy shook her head. "I refuse. She's gone. Caroline is in California. I'm here. Case closed. It doesn't matter."

Footsteps alerted them before Miguel came into the lab. "I could feel your turmoil before I heard your conversation."

"Gods above. Did everyone? This isn't a thing. Caroline's gone and I'm fine. There isn't anything between us."

She didn't realize she was crying until Miguel got close enough to wipe the tears from her cheeks. "I know. We all know. You're a strong, independent woman. You don't need anyone in your life—except maybe that mangy cat of yours."

Mazzy sniffled and laughed. "Yeah, Dennis. I may need him. He's ..." She wasn't sure how to end that sentence.

Miguel wrapped her in a hug. Kaitlyn moved back to where she'd been working earlier. Mazzy leaned in, taking comfort and strength from him, from pack, from all that was alpha.

After a few minutes, he pulled away and gazed into her eyes. "Okay, now, let's talk about what we can do."

What does he think I'm going to do? Run after her like a love-sick pup? "I don't want to leave Colorado. You're my family."

"Good, because I wasn't going to offer that as a suggestion. I was thinking more of a stealth operation to kidnap the alluring witch."

Behind her, Kaitlyn laughed and Mazzy finally relaxed. Her pack was there to support her, and in the end, that was what she needed. He pulled her in for one more hug before releasing her. "You better now?"

"Yeah, I think so. Time to get back to work."

"If you need to go home, just go."

She shook her head. "No, distraction is better."

Kaitlyn's stool scraped on the floor. "Mazzy, I think I have an idea. It's a crazy one, but it just may be the solution we've been looking for."

Chapter 34 - Going Back To Cali
Caroline

Caroline put her last card down and Cinthia took the trick. Everyone counted up their hearts. "I have six points," Caroline said.

Jett smirked. "None for me."

Cinthia sighed, "I have three."

Katt pushed her cards away. "I really don't like this game. I'm bad at it. Seventeen, if you can't do the math. Why do I always end up with the queen of spades?"

Leaning over, Jett kissed her cheek. "You'll learn how to strategize better. You're still new. You're also a bit too nice."

"Whatever. We should go back to playing spades. I like playing with a partner." Katt waggled her eyebrows at Jett, then included the others at the table with a wide smile.

She's really come out of her shell. It's nice to see this side of her. The trip to Colorado did a lot of good for her. Melancholy washed through her at the thought of their trip. *I wonder what Mazzy's doing? Terrorizing someone for leaving a fork out of place? Cuddling with the demon cat? Solving a mystery? Just ... I don't know, being sexy without me?* She sighed. She had to get her head back to California, where it belonged.

Cinthia shook her head. "We decided with a werewolf at the table, Jett had the advantage of being able to read everyone's emotions a bit too well."

With that reminder, Caroline shot a glance at the wolf. Jett was too wrapped up in Katt to be paying attention to her.

Katt tilted her head. "Isn't that the case in any game?"

Jett's smile widened. "It is, but with this one everyone is on their own. A bit more of a Wild West situation."

Cinthia gathered the cards and shuffled. "So, Caroline. You still have all your powers."

Caroline rubbed her face. "Since I've been back, I've tried a few Power of Seven spells, they're easier to cast. I thought that was the case when I tried it in Colorado Springs, but everything there was so off, I wasn't sure if I had been imagining it. But now I'm convinced, it doesn't drain me as much." *Nothing makes sense now that I'm back here without Mazzy.*

Both Katt and Cinthia gaped at her. Katt said, "That's ... important, impressive ... something."

"Yeah, I know. I'm not sure what's happened to me, but I've changed. I'm definitely something different."

Cinthia's eyes narrowed. The coven leader always had the ability to read auras. "Most of you looks the same, but yeah, there's something more. I'll be curious to check you out after the Saturday run ... *if* you run."

A shiver traveled down her back. "Yeah, I'm curious ... and a bit terrified, as well. I mean, what if that's the catalyst that takes away my magic?" *And completes my transformation from witch to wolf ... changing me for good?*

Everyone gazed at her, faces tight with sympathy. The possibility was finally out in the open.

When Caroline had been dropped off the previous night, she'd collapsed into her bed and fallen asleep right away, clothes and all. She'd woken to a call from her coven leader inviting her to breakfast and cards, an offer she couldn't refuse.

After the game, they'd met Tamsin at a local coffee shop with outdoor seating to tell her about what happened. Tamsin asked her to come over Saturday morning. She'd probably be there all day and into the evening for the full moon run. They'd talk more then.

Caroline felt raw and exposed following her chat with the alpha. After lunch, Cinthia took Caroline out grocery shopping, then dropped her off at home.

She felt like she'd lived a few days in one. Her body ached from travel. She trudged through putting away the food. In the fridge she found a pitcher of ... something. It was a golden brown color, a bit cloudy ... *tea maybe?*

Did Cinthia leave this for me while caring for my plants?

Pulling it out, she sniffed it. Her stomach clenched. Yuck. Apple juice. She took a second smell. *Has it gone bad? Is it artificial? Apple juice has never been my favorite, but this smells worse than normal. Stupid wolf senses. Is this what apple juice always smells like? Maybe that's why I've never enjoyed it. Gross!*

With a shrug, she put the coven leader's offering back and continued emptying the grocery sacks.

Jett's words kept playing through her head. It was early afternoon, and Caroline had the rest of the day to herself. Tomorrow she may lose her magic, may lose her status as witch, may stop being everything she'd always been her whole life.

Gah! What will I do then? Will being a werewolf be enough? Will being a professor who howls to the moon be enough? Who am I anymore? I feel like my students, questioning everything about myself, lost. I am way too old for this shit!

Today Caroline wanted to sink into who she'd always been. A pain filled her, down to her soul. She hurt, and needed to find a way to distract herself, something beyond eating ice cream and watching movies. Thinking about students made her think about her lab ... made her want to do something.

Why would Cinthia leave me apple juice? She knows I loathe the stuff. The thought kept interrupting her. Finally, unable to do anything else, she grabbed the apple juice from her fridge and headed to the lab at the college. Kaitlyn had wanted to investigate her blood, why couldn't she?

Once in her lab, she set up everything she needed and got to work. She wasn't sure why she'd decided the apple juice was off, beyond not liking it, but something in her gut didn't like the random juice left behind. *It shouldn't have been in my fridge, and I want to figure out why it was there ... friend or foe.*

Replicating the steps, she and Mazzy had been taking, she lost herself in determining the base compound that made up the liquid.

Even though thinking about the beautiful, sexy werewolf made something in her soul howl, she pushed it away. This was about science, and chemistry was Mazzy's thing. That was the only reason she came to mind. Nothing more than that. *No more thinking about Mazzy outside of the science she inspires.*

While the test ran, she pricked her finger to get a small sample of her blood. The pain radiated to her palm, and she grunted. She put four drops on four separate microscope slides.

On a whim, she put a drop of the apple juice on one of the slides. *The fucking black witches used sweet tea, why not apple juice? I don't know why they'd be after me, except that I was willing to sit in a car with werewolves ... and work with them, oh, and I'm now one of them, and they're fucking crazy.*

As she gazed at the slide, she knew another reason: her coven knew her and her hate of the foul stuff. How dare one of them leave the sludge in her fridge in the first place. It reeked of lazy amateurishness she didn't associate with her people. No one else had access to her home.

Now was the time to shift to science. Like any good scientist, she had the time and was in a mood to try anything.

She set up one of the pure slides in the microscope to study. If not placed in her fridge by one of the evil black witches, she wondered if the apple juice had just gone bad.

Once it was prepped, she went back to the outcome of the analysis of the juice.

Despite everything she'd done, the confirmation of the black witch concoction in the juice hit like a boulder to her gut. Her heart raced. *Someone tried to kill me. Poisoned juice was placed in my refrigerator for me to drink to kill me. Who wants me dead?*

It took her a few minutes to let the shock work its way through her. Her body trembled as she sat there. Shaking out her hands, she knew she had to move. Sitting around wasn't helping anything.

Her blood looked odd. She'd studied witch blood versus human blood over the years, and there was something different about what she looked at now. *I need a sample of werewolf blood. What is wrong with me? Why haven't I studied this in the past? Such a blind spot.*

Next she looked at the combination of her blood and the apple juice. She couldn't make heads nor tails out of what she saw. She wasn't sure what she expected. *The battle for the ages ... and in this corner, the evil apple juice. And in this corner, blood of a witch turned wolf.*

She took another sample of her blood and started on a concoction. It would take a while for it to be ready to test on the apple juice. She could come back on Sunday, assuming she ran tomorrow night. Today, she wouldn't add any magic; she just didn't have the energy.

It was late when she finished. She ordered a pizza from a shop that she normally passed on the way home.

Once she'd picked up her pizza and made it home, she grabbed a beer made by a local brewery from the fridge. What was better with pizza than a cold brew?

While Caroline wolfed down pizza at her dining room table, a knock came to her door. "Come in."

Sage walked in. "You're finally back!"

She wasn't too surprised to see the other witch. They were friendly in the coven, and she'd been back long enough that she expected to see the mini-Cinthia show up.

"I am. I had to return before classes next week. You knew that."

The other woman wore a leather coat. It was cool for Santa Cruz, but after being in a foot of snow, California felt nice. The scent of old leather tickled her nose and she had to hold back a sneeze. *Will I ever get used to all these scents?*

Sage moved to the fridge and peeked in. "Where'd the juice go?" She turned to Caroline with wide eyes. "I made it myself. I had some apples, and I thought you'd like some cider. I thought about adding cinnamon, but then I remembered that you didn't like the stuff. Yesterday it occurred to me, it wasn't the cinnamon you didn't like, but the cider itself." She laughed. "Silly me. Anyway, I came over to grab it and bring it to someone else."

Caroline froze, locking her jaw shut. At the mention of the juice, her heart began to hammer. It took until the end of Sage's blathering for it to slow enough for her to speak. "Apple juice? Huh, my fridge was as empty when I returned as when I left. Don't know what you're talking about. Maybe Cinthia took it, figuring after a week it'd go bad. You know me and the mess this place usually is."

Sage laughed. "Too true, too true. Anyway, just wanted to say 'hi' and I'm glad you're back. We missed you. Will you be at the coven circle tomorrow night?"

Caroline slumped. *Fuck my life!* "No, I'm exhausted from the trip. I'm going to take it easy this weekend and prepare for next week. Speaking of—if you don't mind—I'd like some time alone. I've been with people the entire trip. I haven't had a night alone in over a week."

"Yeah, but that was time with wolves." She visibly shivered. "I'm your people."

The fuck you are! It took everything in Caroline to keep a blank face. "Yeah, I know, but I just need to be alone. You understand. I'll see you later, Sage."

The other woman—the fucking evil black witch—looked hurt, but she shrugged. "I'll bring you more apple cider on Sunday. Would that be okay? Oh, wait, that's right, you don't like it. I could bring you orange juice."

Clenching her jaw tight, she took a second to force herself to answer. "Sure, that would be great."

Chapter 35 - A Human, A Witch, and A Werewolf
Tamsin

Papers were strewn across Tamsin's desk. She sat, hunched, with her head dropped into her hands. Planning for new classes was difficult before the hustle of the semester. She pushed away one stack and pulled a pile with information about the pack. *Two more days and I have to go back to teaching. But I have to survive today first.*

Today was a huge day. Three new wolves ... maybe. Though Cyrus had technically run with them during the last full moon, he was still new. Mil hadn't shifted yet and still carried the scent of a human every time she came to the pack house. Then there was Caroline, a colleague and friend from UC-Santa Cruz.

How will Caroline handle it if she has to shift her sense of self from witch to wolf? If anyone is a proud witch, it's her. She loves playing with her art. If she goes furry today and loses her craft ... it could destroy the woman she is.

A lump developed in Tamsin's gut. *Did they make the right choice?*

Paige came up from behind and wrapped her arms around Tamsin's shoulders. "Relax, everything will be fine. Cyrus is happy and both Mildred and Caroline chose this. Just breathe."

Tamsin relaxed into her mate's embrace as contentment coursed through her. "How do you always know?"

"I'm your partner. Someone has to calm the alpha beast."

"And you volunteered for the ugly job?" Tamsin leaned her head back to look up at her mate.

Paige tightened her hold. "Exactly."

"Okay, my plans for the first week of classes aren't distracting me. Let's go start breakfast."

They headed to the kitchen. Georgette and Maria were there, drinking coffee. Maria smiled. "You're working with the new wolves this morning. We thought you could use some help. Since the rest of the pack will be focused on tonight's run, we're available to help now."

She gave them a small smile. "Thanks. That means a lot."

Tamsin moved to the kitchen to make pancakes and sausage. She knew she had to make a big meal for the wolves' first shift.

Georgette came up next to her. "What can I do to help?"

"How about hash browns? Maria, can you make eggs?"

Maria headed to the fridge. "Sounds good."

The door opened. *It must be Tory with Mildred. I can't see Caroline being bold enough to just walk in yet. She'll learn eventually, that is, if she's a wolf and decides to join our pack.*

Tory walked in, her blue hair bouncing with each step. She had a wide smile on her face. Although she was barely over five feet tall, her personality filled the room. Behind her, Mildred looked just as excited, but Tamsin could sense her apprehension.

Tamsin was about to turn away when she saw Caroline slowly slinking in behind them.

Tory walked to the cupboard with the mugs. "Look who I found sitting outside in a car. I didn't know if she'd come in or sit out there all day, but I figured if she was sitting out there, she could just as easily sit in here and fill her belly."

Caroline sighed. "This is still very new to me. I don't know where I should be, and my mind is all a jumble." She sounded lost.

Tamsin pointed with her chin at the cupboard Tory left open. "Grab a mug, get some coffee. We'll have food ready in a few minutes, then I'll let you all know exactly what my plan is."

Tory and Mildred sat on one side of the table. Caroline sat across from them. The meal didn't take long. As they finished cooking, Cyrus showed up, sitting next to Caroline. He introduced himself with a welcoming smile.

Paige grabbed plates and silverware, then set the table. Once the food was done, Tamsin dished it onto platters, then placed them down in the center of the table. Everyone served themselves, and the room quieted down while they all dug in. When people started refilling their plates, Tamsin determined it was time to lay out her plan for the day.

"The pack runs tonight, and you'll be joining us. As is our tradition, we all eat as a family, a huge dinner. Then we head out. I would like to try to pull out your wolves now, well, after we eat, and have a small run with you before we go as the pack. Get you used to the feel of having fur and paws and running in a group."

Caroline shuddered. "What if nothing happens?"

"I don't know. We try again after dinner. And if nothing happens then we'll try again in a month. At that point, we chalk you up to being weirder than we thought you were before."

Caroline barked out a laugh. "Fair enough."

Though she visibly relaxed, Tamsin could see from how tightly she held her fists and the tremble in her hands that Caroline was still worried.

"Because the process involves nudity, something we get over pretty quickly, I'm going to take you out individually. Once you've shifted, I'll have one of my experienced wolves take you down the trail to our meeting place for the run. It's nice I have so many volunteers this morning."

Cyrus lifted a hand, his excitement vibrating through the bond. "Can I go first?"

Tamsin nodded. "Sounds good"

They headed out to the backyard. Cyrus's face was alight with glee as he looked around at the trees and then up to the sky. He took off his shirt, then turned to face Tamsin. "You know, I know this sounds crazy, but, well, I think my scars kind of went away." He traced his chest.

His scars were only visible if you knew to look for them.

Tamsin couldn't help the huge smile on her face. "That's great."

"But that's not all. I mean, I'm not that different, but I think the rest of me is a bit different, too. It's like the magic of the shift; it's trying to change me. Do you think if I keep shifting—"

"If? You do know it isn't a choice." Tamsin said with a laugh. "Every month, possibly even more often."

"Right. Okay. *As* I keep shifting, could my body change more?"

"I don't know." Tamsin shrugged, but hope filled her. "I'd like you to write things down so we can send what's happening to you to our research facility. I don't know if you're the first, but I doubt you'll be the last."

He nodded. "Yeah, okay, sure."

He turned, finished stripping, and got down on his hands and knees. It took a few minutes, and then a huge, orangish-red male wolf stood in the yard. He started to sniff and investigate.

Tamsin went to collect Georgette.

Next it was Mildred. Tory came out to watch, since Mildred didn't mind. Her shift took a bit longer, but in the end, a dark brown wolf with black markings stood in the backyard. Tory whooped, stripped down, and found her own black wolf. She waited patiently while Mildred sniffed and searched the backyard. After a few minutes she sneezed and looked at Tamsin and Tory. Tamsin could sense through their bond her sheepishness at making them wait. With a small yip, she and Tory were off.

Lastly, it was time for Caroline. She trudged from the house, gnawing on her lower lip. Tamsin had never seen her friend walk so tentatively. "I'm scared, Tamsin."

Tamsin wrapped her arm around the other woman's waist. "I know."

"I don't want to stop being a witch."

"I know."

"Isn't there any way to stop this?" Her voice was soft and held a note of quiet desperation.

"No, my friend. I hope you find peace this day. Regardless of the outcome, you have friends and a family."

She shook her head. "I know. I have other news to share with you, something that happened last night, but … not now."

"Is it important?"

"Yes, but this …. I can't put it off any longer. I have to know."

"Okay." Tamsin gave her one last squeeze. "Okay."

Caroline slowly took off her clothes, as if she were at her own execution. She got down on her hands and knees and dropped her head between her arms, the waterfall of black hair pooling around her hands.

Tamsin put a hand on the base of her head, near her neck, and she could almost hear the wolf within Caroline howling to get out. She wanted to run and be free.

With a small push, and permission to start her journey early, Caroline's body shifted. It was one of the fastest first shifts she'd ever seen. In moments, a giant black wolf stood before her, legs spread, stunning blue eyes wide with shock.

"Go, take in the scents, my friend. I'll get Maria to lead you out."

The wolf didn't move for a few beats, then it shook. Before Tamsin got to the door, the water in a bird bath spiraled up, formed the shape of a heart, and gently landed back in the cement fixture. The wolf woofed, bouncing up. Then it followed a scent, digging its nose deep into a bush.

Tamsin laughed. *Well, that settles that. I will have the oddest pack in the country by far! Two magic-wielding wolves.*

Chapter 36 - The Hills Are Alive
Mazzy

Mazzy sat on her couch cuddling with Dennis. The menace of a cat purred loudly, rubbing his ear against her hand.

She scratched the cat's head and neck as she read over a book on the history of werewolves and their mating. She wasn't sure she believed anything she read, but the anecdotes were plentiful and interesting. Couples that couldn't survive without each other. Love at first sight. They read like the romance section of the library.

"Does anybody believe this?" Mazzy harrumphed.

She sighed and slid the cat over. He hissed and leapt down, circling the room twice, before coming back to lie down exactly where she'd placed him. He glared at her while cleaning his privates.

"Yeah, yeah, have fun with your neutered self. I have to go meet the pack. You'll be on your own for the night, big man. If you go out, text, so I don't come home to an empty house. I'm trusting you to be safe."

She smiled as she gathered her boots, coat, and bag. It was cold out there, but the moon called, and she wanted nothing more than to shed her humanity and stretch her muscles.

More than any month she could remember in a while, she needed the feel of being a wolf and running on her four paws, her pack around her, and the wind in her fur. She felt confined in her skin, and wanted to howl.

She drove out to Cheyenne Mountain State Park, where the pack would be running this month. There were a bunch of cars. When they came out to the national park to shift, they'd meet about a mile out at a shelter where they could drop their belongings. Miguel always brought a generator and a heated tent for their clothes. It was nice to not have to put on frozen items after the run.

She found everyone at the shelter, a fire in a permanent grill, food sizzling, beer in a cooler, and talk and laughter in the wind. Mazzy approached with a smile. Alice handed her a plate and a can as she started to join her pack family.

Once everyone arrived, the fire was put out, the rubbish was cleaned away, and everyone began shifting. Mazzy wasn't always the first to go furry, but today she needed her wolf. The pain felt cathartic. Quicker than it had ever happened, she stood on four paws. Gazing up at the clear black sky filled with sparking stars and the large moon, she howled her pain at missing Caroline.

Miguel, also in wolf form, came up to rub against her.

While the others finished, Mazzy trotted off and found a trail of a feral cat. She followed it until it went up a tree.

Others from the pack joined her, and they ran. Her muscles sang as the miles flew by. They were shadows in the trees, save for the howls of delight. Miguel touched her mind.

"Are you doing better? You feel like you're letting go."

Mazzy howled, scaring a nearby squirrel from a tree. *"I don't know. My body is fine, but my soul feels torn up. I don't understand what's going on."*

"There's only one solution. It's obvious. Alice and I discussed it last night. I'll tell you tomorrow morning. We have a gift for you. We'll meet you in the lab at eight a.m. with Kaitlyn."

Mazzy tried to get more out of him, but he was gone from her mind, their connection there, but silent. She shook her head and ran.

The wind brought her the scent of deer. The others were already veering in that direction. Miguel directed the pack. Mazzy was in the back, a chaser. She would help tire out the prey while others would bring it down once it slowed.

When she was told to stop, she did. Others were more fierce. Miguel knew each member's strengths, and Mazzy's was of the mind.

Another chase. The deer's haunches pumping with its fast breathing, Gus and Miguel leapt and tackled the large animal down. In turns, they each took some of the meat.

With the heat of the hunt still on her tongue and in her blood, Mazzy headed back alongside the others to their base, where they reclaimed their humanity. In the cooler with the beer there was also water and soda. Some went for the beer, though Mazzy wanted water.

The snow melted under her feet, the cold sending tendrils up her legs as a shiver shook her body despite her werewolf metabolism. Winter in Colorado in human form was intense. She found her clothes and dressed before she froze. On her way out, Kaitlyn found her. "Do you know why Miguel wants us at the lab tomorrow morning? It's Sunday. He never wants to work on a Sunday."

"No idea, but we need to check our solutions, so we'll do that, then head out for brunch. Sounds like a great day to me." They'd made it to the full parking lot, finishing their conversation.

Kaitlyn rolled her eyes. "Yeah, well, you have an odd sense of what makes a good day, don't you?"

Opening the door to her car, Mazzy winked. "Science is sexy, Kaitlyn, and you know it!"

Her friend just snorted as she got into her own car.

Chapter 37 - A Solution
Caroline

The sun cut across Caroline's eyes, waking her up. She stretched, wiggling, trying to find a comfortable position. In the last week, she'd lost count of the number of different beds she'd slept in, and once again, she missed her own house.

After she'd shifted the first time, the scents overwhelmed her. In the backyard there were trees and flowers, the garden became a whole new world to her wolf's nose. She didn't want to leave when Maria nudged her.

On the path to the meeting spot, she smelled cats, a slew of cats. The memory of Mazzy cut through her, and she whimpered. She stopped, sticking her nose in the dead tree she thought the cats used for a home. Her whimpering continued as she snuffled the area.

She felt Maria near her, but she kept digging her nose in, not caring about the other wolf. She wanted to see the cats. She wasn't sure why. They wouldn't be orange, they wouldn't be Dennis, they wouldn't bring Mazzy, but ... she just needed the connection.

Tamsin's voice came into her head. *"Caroline, you need to move on. What you're looking for isn't here."*

"I need ... I ... what's happening to me?"

"Let's run, it'll help."

They got into the open area and her body sang with the movement. In between the runs, Caroline told Tamsin about Sage. She wasn't one hundred percent sure, but close to it. They planned on talking to Cinthia after Tamsin could confirm. Apparently the wolves now had a way to scent-test for black witches.

Later that night, after dinner and during the second run, everything was even better. Becoming one with the pack was beyond anything Caroline could imagine.

She would go home, not stay in this room they gave her at the pack house, and some time this week she would work with Cinthia to test her magic. She'd tried the one water spell as a wolf, and it had worked. She could still feel the power within her, but she had to do more. The coven leader could do a more thorough test than Katt had done, and Caroline had to know.

She also wanted to go to the lab and analyze her solution. It was a long shot, but she couldn't be still. Every time she stopped moving, the pain came back. Tomorrow, school started, and that would help, but today ... today she had to distract herself.

I wonder if Mazzy has thought of me once since I left. No! Stop. Don't think that way. Mazzy has a job and a life in Colorado. If she's thinking about you, then it's connected to these damn black witches. Focus on that.

Caroline got up and showered. On the main level of the pack house, a gaggle of wolves prepared a feast for brunch. She tried to leave, but her stomach growled.

After taking her place at the kitchen table, she ate a plate stacked with food. Jett, seated across from her, smiled. "Are you ready for tomorrow?"

"Not even slightly. I was going to prep for this week's classes over the weekend, and I haven't been home yet."

"Ditto. I'm heading to the dorms after this. A bit of quiet downtime should do the trick."

Caroline nodded. "Do you want a ride? I have something I need to check in the lab."

"Sure! That would be great. Twenty minutes?"

With a relieved sigh, Caroline nodded.

Next to Jett, Paige sipped her coffee. "So, construction starts this week. It will be done by spring break, when the wedding is planned. I am so excited. Will you be available at all to talk to the construction crew?"

Jett nodded. "Yeah. I've already spent some time on Friday getting them up to speed, but I'll be dropping in a few times a week to monitor their work. Don't worry, your suite will be exactly what you want."

Paige's smile was dazzling. "Thank you, Jett. You don't know how much we appreciate this."

It amused Caroline how much Tamsin had talked about the renovation the previous quarter at school. She was excited for her and Paige.

They finished their meal and said their good-byes. The ride to campus was quiet. Both women were absorbed with their own thoughts.

After parking and waving goodbye to Jett, Caroline went to the lab to check on her solution. It seemed to work. She ran the tests twice, the second time recording everything with her phone on video mode. Once she confirmed the success, she emailed the video to Mazzy with images of her lab notes. If they could replicate it, then maybe they had their solution. Excitement surged through her, making her body feel electric.

I did it! I figured it out! I solved the unsolvable puzzle. She stopped her thoughts and gazed down at her body with its limited blood. *Am I enough to solve this?*

She cleaned the lab and headed back to her car, finally feeling drained enough she may get a good night's sleep. She was ready to go home. Being in an empty house was probably a bad idea, but she couldn't think of anyone she wanted to be with. Well, she could, but that someone was half a country away, probably snuggling with an impertinent orange cat.

Lost in thought, she parked her car in front of her house and sat for a few minutes. She didn't want to be alone, but she didn't want to be with people. She just didn't want ... anything. *Gods, I miss her. I do want something. And what I want comes with an obnoxious orange cat.*

She closed her eyes and let the conflicting emotions flow through her as she tried to bite back the tears that pricked her eyes.

Why is this so bloody hard? Just get out of the freaking car, go into your house, and open a bottle of wine. Turn on the TV and lose yourself in the miasma of wine and a bad Hallmark romance. Come on, Caroline, you can do it.

A knock on her window had her jumping in her seat.

Before she opened her eyes, she thought, *If it's Sage, I'm biting off her head, and damn the consequences.*

Finally opening her eyes, she looked over and saw brown curly hair and brown eyes. Joy surged through her as she opened the door. "I've been waiting on your stoop, and you finally get here, and you won't leave your car. What's wrong with you?"

Caroline's mouth gaped open, and she wasn't sure she could do anything about it. *Am I hallucinating? Dreaming? Did I conjure an image of my deepest want? Can I even do that?* She was distracted for a moment, thinking about if the Power of Seven could even do any of it.

Mazzy reached over with a finger and gently pushed her jaw shut. "Hi. You okay with me being here?" A warm smile spread across her face.

Caroline nodded. "More than okay. Are you really here, or did I bang my head and fall into a really good dream?"

"Hmm," Mazzy hummed. "I like being called your dream woman. But, alas, I'm really here. Dennis is in a cat carrier, ready to kill me."

"Dennis?" Caroline wasn't sure how much more she could take. "Really? Like, for real?"

"Can we go in and take this from the top? I have my own questions for you. As well as some information."

"Yes. Absolutely. Mi casa es tu casa." *Forever and ever, if it were my choice.*

"Good, I'm going to hold you to that." The sexy wolf winked.

Chapter 38 - Cat Nip
Mazzy

Mazzy clutched her bags to her chest as she looked through Caroline's front door. She could see into the woman's kitchen. It wasn't dirty, but there was clutter everywhere. *Is this how she lives? Can I stay here? Will she want me to stay here?*

The thought of going anywhere else made her wolf snarl, and she knew she'd have to figure out how to cohabitate with someone who didn't live as tidily as she did. *Admit it, Mazzy, you've fallen for a brilliant slob!*

She shivered at the thought.

Caroline smiled at her, eyes dancing. "Welcome, Mazzy. Enter in peace."

The way the other woman said the words ... there had to be some meaning behind them. "Um, thanks?"

A humorless laugh preceded Caroline shaking her head. "Sorry, it's a traditional witch's welcome. I don't even know why I said it."

"Ah," Mazzy nodded. "Habit. How should I respond?"

"The traditional response is, 'Thank you, Caroline, or rather name of host, I enter in peace and hope for nothing but tranquility for you and yours.'"

Mazzy furrowed her brows as she thought about the words. "There is more to it than the words, aren't there? When witches say it, they push out some of their power. A promise to behave."

"A bit. Katt and I were impressed that Miguel knew the ceremony."

Shocked, Mazzy gaped at her. "Really? You did this before entering the pack house? Wait, I thought you didn't go there. No, you met everyone before meeting me, that first night. You went there then."

"Yes to all of that."

"Okay, so, Thank you, Caroline, I enter in peace and ..."

"Hope for—"

Mazzy waved her one free hand. "Hope for nothing but tranquility for you and yours."

Caroline waved her hand in welcome. "You can drop your stuff in the living room. I'll get a pot of water up for ... tea? Coffee? Beer? Wine? Water? What do you want?"

"I wouldn't mind a beer, depending on what you have."

Mazzy stacked her stuff in the living room. "Do you mind if Dennis explores? He's traveled with me before and as long as he has a litter box, he behaves."

"Did you come that prepared?" Caroline asked, gaping at Mazzy's stuff.

"Sure did. Wouldn't bring my cat without his box." Her smile was sheepish.

"Well, then that should be fine. He won't eat all my plants, will he?"

"Ah, I don't actually know. If he does, we can figure out a solution."

After freeing her companion, Mazzy headed to the kitchen and found Caroline waiting for her with a cold beer and a plate with sliced cheese and salami. There was a side table against the wall covered with papers. She wondered if Caroline just dumped everything from the main table over to the smaller side table. She shrugged before digging in. "Thank you."

"So, not that I'm not a bit thrilled that you're here, but to what do I owe this surprise?"

"Before we jump into that, can I ask how last night went?"

Caroline blanched. "Yeah ... about that. I guess I'm a complete anomaly."

"Did anyone get a picture? I'd love to see your wolf."

Color quickly returned to Caroline's face as she blushed. "From what I was told, I'm black as night."

Mazzy smiled. "Nice. Sexy."

Caroline laughed. "Tamsin gave me a room at pack house and extended an invitation to her pack. She spoke in my mind and everything. I just ... it's so much. School starts tomorrow, and I'm more excited about the diversion than I can tell you. Part of me wishes I was back in your lab, hiding from so many changes."

"I mean, it's always an option." Mazzy reached over, placing her hand on Caroline's arm.

"Not really. I have so many responsibilities here. Not only my job ... I think I figured it out. I sent you a video, did you get it?" Her voice pitched up at the end with her excitement.

Mazzy's eyebrows rose. "Did you, now? I haven't checked my phone, no. I was on a plane, then trying to figure out how to get here."

"That's right, you're sitting in my house, in Santa Cruz, with your cat. You have your own story." Caroline lifted her bottle and realized it was empty. "Need a refill?"

Mazzy nodded. Hers was still half full, but she figured she may as well get a head-start and not interrupt the flow or their talk. "Kaitlyn had the idea of testing your crazy blood. It's crazy, but it's the key. You're the key. You're the one who'll break this stronghold, save your city."

"Yeah, that's what I figured out, too. It's why I have to stay here. But what are you doing here?" An intensity flowed from Caroline, like she wanted to ask more, but was afraid to.

"I'm here to set up a remote lab. I'm going to mass produce the concoction from Sunrise Pharmaceutical so that it can go out to EMTs, emergency departments, and any other medical organizations that may face random heart attacks. It doesn't take much of your blood, but given the number of places the concoction needs to go and the amount of blood you can donate, we'll have to produce the antidote slowly. I figure I'll be here for a few months." She paused and bit her bottom lip. "I need a place to stay. I was hoping I could stay here."

The look of joy that crossed Caroline's face was all the answer Mazzy needed. She knew they'd need to work out compromises, but they didn't need to worry about how they felt about each other.

Caroline tilted her head. "Wait, does that mean your research division, the hidden center that doesn't produce anything, is suddenly going live? You're going to actually produce tangible results?"

Mazzy lifted her beer in salute. "Alice is scrambling to figure out how to spin an area of the company most of the shareholders didn't know existed suddenly going out into the world making a splash."

"Will you label it under a different division?"

"Eh, above my pay-grade. I'm just going to do the science. The rest is up to my alphas."

Chapter 39 - One Is The Loneliest Number
Caroline

Spring Break

Caroline lay in bed, half asleep. Her mind wandered over the last few assignments she needed to grade and record before the school's deadline. Her heart pounded faster, keeping her from falling back asleep.

Pointy daggers poked her, starting at her ankles, working its heavy way up her legs, to her hip, over her waist to her shoulder, where something furry and warm finally plopped down. A vibrating motor in her ear finally roused her fully.

"Come on, Dennis, let a witch sleep, will you? I know I have papers to grade."

A groan from next to her warmed her to her soul. Sharing a bed, a home, a life with Mazzy had been more than she'd hoped for. "No, you don't. It's spring break. You submitted everything yesterday. You even donated blood, so we have the day off to play."

"I submitted ... I ... oh! Yeah. The end of the quarter is always weird. One week off for good behavior, and it's back to the grind."

Mazzy rolled over to give her a kiss. "You know. It's been three months. We've done a lot building the new lab and starting production on the antidote for the heart attack victims. According to Mildred, we've already saved a few people. But I don't think you can donate enough blood."

Caroline rolled to her back, dislodging the cat who tried to stay on her, but ended up jumping to the floor with a thump. "I'm doing the best I can. I'm not sacrificing all of myself for the good of the people of Santa Cruz. What if something like this happens again?"

"I don't know. I think we need to speak with Tamsin."

Caroline sighed, but knew Mazzy was right. "Okay, let's get up, eat, and I'll call the alpha. If she's around and has time. She and Paige are getting married on Friday."

"I don't get that. Why now? Why not wait until summer?"

"I'm surprised she waited this long and didn't take a page from Maria and Blake's playbook and elope." Caroline narrowed her eyes and let her mind run away with images of her and Mazzy slipping off to Vegas together. With a shake of her head, she sighed. *What am I thinking? We're just trying to get this black magic shit eradicated ... why am I thinking long term?*

Mazzy laughed. "Fair enough."

They decided to go to a café nearby. Caroline ordered a large omelet with a side of pancakes and hashbrowns. She didn't make the call until her food was gone, figuring anything could wait until her stomach stopped growling at her. She'd spent so much time in awe of the werewolves' appetite; now that she had one herself, she enjoyed the flavors, but sometimes wondered if she'd always be a servant to her belly.

She tried Tamsin's number, but it went to voicemail, as did Paige's when Caroline called her next. Caroline finally tried Georgette. "I'm at work today, but from what I understand, it's a madhouse over there. Then again, it always is. But, Caroline, you're pack, you don't need permission, just go. And for the love of Pete, don't knock or ring the bell. For once, be *pack* and just walk in."

Georgette hung up before Caroline could respond.

Mazzy slid her arm around Caroline's shoulder. "She's not wrong. It's wild to me to watch you formally knock on your own pack door. You're part of the family now, act like it."

Caroline squeezed her eyes shut, then rubbed her face. "Okay, fine. Let's go. It still feels wrong to the witch side, but the wolf in me agrees wholeheartedly."

When they got to the pack house, Caroline metaphorically pulled up her big-girl panties and walked in.

In the living room, a group sat drinking coffee and talking. Tamsin glanced up at her with a huge smile. "About time! Want to see the new ensuite?"

Caroline wanted to kick herself. *How could I forget it was done this week? They'd been talking about that for months. Paige's gift. Jett's design. It was the biggest thing that'd happened around here since ... well, in the last year a lot of big things had happened.*

While Caroline's mind reeled at her obvious lack of memory, Mazzy pushed her forward. "Of course we would."

Paige led the way. "The bedroom didn't change, though the office area did. If you see, the desk goes along two walls with plenty of outlets for any type of electronics."

The dark wooden desk was magnificent, and the lighter wall with windows that overlooked the backyard made the room bright. There were framed pictures on two of the walls. Caroline only recognized some of the people.

"Then over here," Paige continued the tour. "Through our bedroom is the bathroom."

Caroline's mind stuttered to a stop. She wasn't sure if she was amazed, impressed, or envious. All she knew was, one day, she wanted to live in that room. "Whoa."

"I know, right. When Jett showed me her ideas, I had no idea she could actually pull them off."

The door opened up to a bathroom with white and gray tile on the floor and walls. It had two separate vanities, one on the left, one on the right. Since the room had to be at least ten feet across, there was plenty of space if both vanities were in use at the same time. The counter and sink were a black marble with white veining and sat on oak, open-shelf bases. There were arched doorways beyond the vanity.

Through the left was a walk-in closet that had an island in the center for shoes, scarves, and jewelry. The alcove to the right contained the toilet.

The far end of the ensuite was a large arch highlighting the 'wet' area of the room. On the other side was a shower room with multiple shower heads to one side. When Caroline walked in to count how many, she saw a full jacuzzi tub that would easily fit two comfortably tucked away on the other side.

She slowly turned to face Mazzy and saw the same look of desire on her face. Paige smiled at them both. "I know, it's fantastic. I'm thinking about coming in here, shutting the door, and never leaving."

Mazzy snapped her mouth shut. "I wouldn't blame you. I want to hide in here and never leave. I'm pretty sure I could hide and not be found for a few days."

Paige laughed.

Back out in the living room, they sat on a couch and faced Tamsin. She smiled at them. "How goes the antidote production?"

Mazzy shrugged. "Good, but our main sticking point is that I don't think Caroline can safely supply enough blood. I had no idea the amount the hospitals and medical facilities around here would request. She can donate a liter of blood every three to four weeks, more than a human, but I'm not going to push it beyond that."

Tamsin nodded. "I wouldn't ask you to. This is about saving lives, not taking them. I worried about not having enough of the key ingredient. I know the demand will be dropping, but I'm sure there's a lot of stock out there right now."

Paige slumped. "Is there anything we can do?"

"No." Caroline sighed. "It was such a specific set of circumstances, we aren't even sure what exactly caused it. Was it the black magic and Power of Seven getting into my blood? Was it that, combined with the bite? Was it my being a witch? Was it me being in

Colorado? Was it something with Mazzy? There are too many factors."

Katt walked out of the kitchen with Jett. "We could recreate all but one of those. We aren't in Colorado Springs, but everything else is reproducible."

Jett shook her head. "The process could also kill you."

"It's more likely to cause me to lose my magic."

"And that isn't acceptable either." Jett turned Katt to face her. "I've seen you doing magic in a way no one else has. You ... you and your magic are intertwined. I don't think you know what you're talking about losing."

Katt's face was hard as she said, "Jett, this is people's lives. I can't be so selfish to say my life is worth more than theirs."

Caroline worried for Katt, but couldn't be prouder of her former student and coven sister.

Tamsin swiveled to search Katt's face. "This isn't a small decision, Katt. I can't tell you 'yes' or 'no.' I don't even feel comfortable advising you beyond this: I think you should talk to your family. Your mom fought a lot to get you where you are today."

Katt nodded. "Okay, that's reasonable."

It took another two days, but Katt was determined. She'd probably made up her mind on the car ride back from Colorado when she'd heard about Caroline's accident. Her mom was against it, but her dad supported her. He explained her mom would come around and no matter what, she'd love Katt to the ends of the earth and back again.

They went to the lab that Mazzy had set up. They'd brought Tory, because she was a nurse, and having someone who knew medicine would be helpful.

Using the notes from December, they recreated the concoction from the black magic poisoned apple juice, Mazzy's blood, and the Power of Seven spell used all those months ago. They created four samples.

After twenty-four hours, both Mazzy and Caroline smelled each one. One smelled off and Caroline was about to toss it, when Mazzy shook her head. "No, that's the one we have to use. The one that worked smelled off. I almost forgot."

They got everything set up for Katt, and Mazzy shifted to wolf.

They combined the juice and mixture in a metal box that would contain any explosions. They heard a muffled sound. Once combined, they immediately injected Katt, who lay on the floor wearing her bikini.

"Gods, the room is getting wonky. Did that happen to you? Like it spun and was wobbly?"

Jett looked at Caroline, her brows furrowed. Caroline reached out and squeezed her hand. "Breathe. I'm sure she's going to be okay. She wants this."

"That's part of the problem. She's changing herself for me. It's ... it's a lot." Jett dropped her head. "Maybe too much."

"No." Caroline shook her head, her voice coming out solid. "She's doing this for herself and our community." She smirked. "You're just a side effect, barely a second thought, I'm sure."

Though Jett could probably hear the partial lie, Jett was definitely important to Katt. Jett's shoulder's dropped and she let out a sigh. "Thanks, that helps."

Tory ducked in and pulled some of Katt's blood. Caroline tested it. It felt like the testing took forever. Finally, the results came in. "Positive for the black magic concoction."

On the floor, Katt smiled. "Good. Okay, Jett, please leave. You can come back afterwards."

"No."

"Yes. Leave, now." There was such power in her voice, Jett wavered.

Caroline moved up to her former student. "Come on, let's go get some food. She'll need to eat as soon as she's cleaned up."

Jett snarled, but nodded. They headed across the street and picked up sandwiches, chips, fruit, and drinks. When they returned, Katt lay on the ground, shaking, but bandaged. Mazzy had already cleaned up the blood.

They ate, and then Tory took another blood sample for Caroline to test. "It's clean."

Mazzy ran some more tests while Tory checked the wounds. "She's healing."

"Her blood matches yours. After the full moon next week, we should be able to start getting donations from her as well as you."

Caroline sighed as relief slammed into her like a wrecking ball knocking down a building. She hadn't realized how stressed she'd been about being the only blood source for the cure. Suddenly, she felt like an end was at sight ... a successful end.

Chapter 40 - A Whole New World
Mazzy

All Mazzy's bags were packed. They were piled in the living room ready to head back to Colorado Springs. She was going home. Excitement bubbled up in her at the thought of returning to her apartment, her pack, her job.

She'd enjoyed Santa Cruz, the ocean, the beach, getting to know the Pacific Pack wolves, and avoiding the snow, but she missed her own family. She missed the mountains. She missed the volunteer work and the routines she'd established over the years.

The new lab she'd set up was good. Miguel and Alice had decided to keep it up and running as an extension of the company, just under other management, staffed by a different scientist. Mazzy missed her own state-of-the-art facility that Miguel had built. The one with Kaitlyn, Gus, and Thomas.

Both the local pack and the coven were holding a final goodbye meal at the pack house. An affair she looked forward to and feared. She couldn't imagine that many people in one place. It would be ... overwhelming.

Caroline came up behind her and wrapped her in a hug. "Ready to go?"

Mazzy turned and gave her a kiss. "No, but if you're there, I'll survive."

The celebration was more than a goodbye, it was a thank you for all the work she'd done. She couldn't believe the amount of antidote they'd made. With the addition of Katt's blood, they'd stockpiled enough to hopefully last the summer, if any more heart attacks showed up. The process had reached a point where she was no longer needed on site if more was required.

She and Caroline drove to pack house, leaving Dennis free until after the meal. The place was ready to burst with people. Everyone gave hugs, and there were tears. Werewolves were much more affectionate than regular humans. Caroline headed off to find Tamsin.

Katt came up to her, a gleam in her eyes. "Thank you so much. I know I've thanked you like a million times, but I can't believe it all worked."

Mazzy gave her a hug. *Gods above, witches all over the place. What is happening to me? And I'm choosing to hug them? My pack will die when they hear about this.* "You helped save your city. You helped stop the black witches, which was your right. *I* should be thanking *you*. Your parents should be proud. I know your mom is still hurt, but she'll come around. Make sure to visit when you're home."

"Oh, I will. I'm heading to Denver for a month this summer, and I plan on harassing you and your pack at least every full moon. Maybe even more than that."

Warmth blossomed in Mazzy, another shock. She'd grown fond of the young witch, even before she'd become a wolf. "Good."

Cinthia came up to Mazzy and kissed her on each of her cheeks. "You're a good person, Mazzy Sinclair. It has been a pleasure getting to know you over the last few months, even with your prickly opinions about witches."

Mazzy blushed. She'd tried to tamp down her opinions, especially around the coven leader. She felt her cheeks warm as she mumbled. "I'm sorry if I was rude."

"No worries. I just hope you and Caroline are happy. You're taking away one of my best witches ... and best friends. I know she'll be happy with you in Colorado Springs, and the job sounds perfect for her. You're perfect for her. She's needed a bit of a shake up for a while.

Do stay in touch. You all have a family or two here as well as there."

Tears pricked her eyes as she nodded. "Of course. There's no way we wouldn't stay in touch. And I'm as surprised as you that she decided to quit teaching and follow me home." As if a force beyond her pulled at them, Mazzy met Caroline's gaze across the room, and they shared a small smile.

Cinthia smiled. "I'm not."

The meal and celebration was ... epic. So many people, so much food—excellent food. By the time they extracted themselves, returned to Caroline's house, which was already on the market, and got their stuff, they were ready to get into the truck and on the road.

The start of the journey was rough. Dennis apparently didn't love city driving. He yowled at every red light. Caroline leaned over to Mazzy. "Is he offering himself up as a mid-travel snack?"

She swatted Caroline. In her heart, she knew the other woman teased, but Dennis was her baby. "Not funny."

"Oh, hilarious." At the next red light, instead of eyeing the mewling cat, Caroline kissed Mazzy's cheek. "We could also give him a sedative."

"Once we get on the interstate, he'll be fine."

She flopped back. "Okay, not a snack, just background white noise ... or cat noise, got it?"

Mazzy watched as the trees flew by. The warmth rekindled in her heart toward the witch-turned-wolf seated beside her. Her partner in science and in love. Twenty hours or more and they'd be home.

Find the Next Book

Lupine Investigation, here:
https://mybook.to/LupineInvestigation

Or the final Novela: Honey Moon here:

https://mybook.to/HoneyMoon

Where to Find Harlowe Frost
Thanks for reading!
Find more of my books on my website:
http://hannahwillowauthor.com

You can also find me on:
Twitter: @hannahwillow217
Instagram: @hannahwillow217
Facebook Hannah Willow

About the Author

Harlowe Frost has been a teacher at both the high school and college level. Her parents instilled a love of reading from a young age. She grew up in the queer community. Her favorite genre growing up was fantasy and science fiction, that is, until she discovered urban fantasy and paranormal romance. What she never found in those books was the diversity in background, gender identity, and sexuality she saw in the people around her. She decided if she couldn't find that in what she read, then she would write it herself. This started her writing paranormal romance with a LGBTQ+ background